The Valley of Yeshen

Descent to War

C. J. Korryn

Published by C. J. Korryn Books 2023

Published by:

C. J. Korryn Books

****

©2023 by C. J. Korryn

****

Connect with C. J. Korryn

Learn more about C. J. Korryn at his author website, **cjkorryn.com** where you can sign up for his monthly newsletter, discover his other books, follow him on social media, and much more.

Chapter One

Leo stood over his baldric and axes massaging the back of his neck, then rubbed his furry white cheeks and whiskers, thankful to finally be setting out. The council had at last come to a decision. A decision that he would have made—did make—in minutes. He hated being summoned to council meetings and was grateful they very seldom happened. The council only convened when the priest-king was not available, which was, indeed, rarely. Now was one of those times. He was finally preparing for his quest, a journey he would have liked to have started days ago. However, without the priest-king to lead his people, it fell to the council, which always took too long to make decisions.

He was of the cat kind, the Feleine, a rare race that lived in the mountains and seldom ventured far from the confines of their lands. His fur was predominantly orange with black stripes and white around his nose, mouth, and paw-like hands. His nose was solid black, and his eyes were green, especially unusual for cat folk.

He wore thick leather boots and leather cuirass armor that covered his chest and back, which was strapped to a simple leather fauld made of a heavy belt with large, overlapping flaps of leather that hung to mid-thigh.

Leo snatched up his matching leather baldric, the weapon's holster specially tailored for carrying his battle-axes, and slid it over his head. He strapped the baldric to the shoulder of his cuirass, then to his fauld on the opposite side, so it lay across his chest. After ensuring the straps were tight, he grabbed his two small battle-axes and slid them into the blade holsters on his baldric, one on his back, the other in front, and set off to meet with the others joining him on his mission.

He grabbed his traveling pack and headed out the door, snatching his gray cloak on the way out and shoving it into his overstuffed traveling bag. He had packed what gear he knew he would need for the dangerous journey. If there was one thing his many years of hunting and traveling had taught him, it was always to be prepared, so he packed clothing for every weather condition he could think of.

"Leorneth, we thought you might have lost your spine!" hollered Slarnath as Leo neared, standing to greet him. Slarnath was one of Leo's oldest and closest friends. The two were like brothers. Leo knew that Slarn, as they called him, would die for him, as he would die for Slarn.

Slarn wore the same gear as Leo: a baldric worn across the chest, a cuirass, and a fauld covering his midsection. He was all black: his fur, his eyes, his nose, his whiskers, everything. Looking at Slarn was like looking into a dark hole.

"Not today, Slarn. Not today," Leo replied.

7

Flanking Slarn were Morlithis and Fieraneth. Morlithis had a coat of many colors, splotched sporadically with white, black, yellow, and gray, and Fieraneth, a female warrior, had pure white fur. They wore the same warrior's gear as Slarn and Leo. Like Leo, Fieraneth wielded their people's traditional weapon, the battle-axe, one strapped to the front of her baldric and one strapped high onto her back, so her pack she carried didn't hinder her access to the axe. Unlike Leo, however, Morlithis and Slarn carried other weapons. Slarn's weapons of choice were long knives, and Morlithis's was a crossbow, though he also kept a small battle-axe for close combat.

"Well, then, let's get going, shall we?" Fieraneth suggested. They all nodded, and the four headed out for their mission to save the priest-king, each with their own small bundle of supplies strapped to their backs.

The team of four traveled through the dense forest until nightfall, and Leo, Slarn, and Fiera, as they called her, set up camp and prepared a fire while Morlithis caught their meal with his bow and arrow. Not long after the camp and fire were set, Morlithis returned with a haul of rabbits and squirrels. Soon, the four were enjoying fresh-cooked meat.

"Tomorrow, we should reach the edge of the Yeshen Valley," Leo reported. "We will have to be on our guard while in the valley. It is a very dangerous region," he finished.

"Have you been through the region before?" asked Morlithis.

"He sure has," Slarn answered, replying for Leo. "It was not a pleasant experience, but those were bad times, and things are no longer as bad."

"Not *as* bad," Leo added. "Still bad."

"Well, we all need to get some good sleep tonight," Slarn said, standing up and retiring to his bedroll. "When we are in the Yeshen Valley, we will need to take turns on watch. It should be safe enough here that we don't need to worry about keeping watch." The three soon followed suit, quickly falling asleep after setting out their bedrolls.

The next morning, the four woke at the break of dawn; they rolled up their sleeping rolls, doused the remnants of the smoldering fire, and headed to the Yeshen Valley.

They traveled most of the day in the familiar surroundings of the forest, venturing past their own borders soon after leaving camp and into the seldom-traveled outskirts of the forest.

Rarely did the Feleine people venture more than a day's journey from their villages. However, it was their last-ditch effort to save their priest-king, and desperate times called for desperate measures. He lay deathly ill, and the healer had exhausted all of his vast knowledge of healing herbs and potions but could not heal him. The healer had mentioned to the council that there was a possibility that a rare herb that grew in the Yeshen Valley might be potent enough to cure the priest-king, so the four were sent to find it and bring it back.

Toward the late hours of the afternoon, the party reached the Yeshen Valley, where the forest abruptly stopped at a sheer cliff overlooking the valley. It was deceptively beautiful, with mountains surrounding it and a visible river slicing through the valley's center. The trees seemed even greener than those of the forest, and the air smelled fresher. They knew this to be because of the nearby waterfall. The wind carried the waterfall's mist to them, coating their fur with a cold, thin layer of droplets. The roar of the falling water was not too loud, as it was several hundred yards away.

"It is beautiful," said Fiera.

"Indeed, it is," replied Slarn. "But we must keep our guard up now. It is not as pleasant as it appears, and we have a long way to go."

"There is a cave we can camp in behind the waterfall," Leo reported. The three nodded, and they made their way to the waterfall. The closer they came, the heavier their fur grew as the mist accumulated, soaking them. They reached the edge of the waterfall, its roar now deafening. Leo neared the edge of the cliff, glancing down before turning around and waving for the others to follow, but as he waved them over, he slipped, falling over the edge.

Chapter 2

Morlithis and Fiera rushed over to the edge as Slarn laughed, drowned out by the water's roar. Leo knelt on a lower ledge, looking up at the two and smiling. Morlithis and Fiera both replied with a sneer, not amused by Leo's practical joke. Leo stood up, took a steadying hold of the edge, and began slowly shimmying to the right, disappearing behind a wall of falling water. Slarn hopped down and followed, as did Morlithis and Fiera.

They stood on the rock ledge facing the cliff with the waterfall to their backs. Leo led the four down a sloping path that zigzagged back and forth from one side of the waterfall to the other. The progress was slow but steady. Fiera and Morlithis noticed hand grips carved into the cliffside through the more difficult sections of the climb down. This confirmed, in their minds, the question the two had been silently asking themselves: Had this path been made, or was it natural?

They had finally reached the bottom of the waterfall, which held a deep cavern behind the cold sheet of water. They had to wade through a thigh-deep pool to get to a dry portion of the massive cave, but they were already soaked to the bone, so none of them thought twice about it.

"I hate getting wet," Fiera complained once they were finally on the dry surface of the cave.

"Don't we all?" Slarn replied. The four shook off the excess water from their fur as best they could, flinging it in all directions.

"Morlithis, we're going to need some firewood and dinner," Leo said. "You can use the small opening over there to come and go." He pointed to the corner of the cave, just past the opening behind the waterfall from which they entered. "Fiera will go with you. We need firewood first.

Get a lot of wood. After that, you can hunt for food. Slarn and I will make sure the cave is safe while you are gathering wood."

Thanks to their night vision that granted them sight even in the depths of the cavern's blackness with little light, they quickly determined the cave vacant and returned to the entrance to prepare the fire while Fiera and Morlithis hunted.

***

"So, remind me again what this special herb is called and why it's so special," Morlithis requested as he bit into a large piece of cooked rabbit.

Slarn tossed a sliver of meat at him. "Weren't you listening at all during the council meetings?" he replied.

"It's called catnip. It is very potent," added Fiera. "We need to get as much of it as possible to take back."

"It has extraordinarily strong healing properties," Leo reported. "It can only be found down here, but not many want to risk their lives for it, though it is precious. If anything can heal King Phrenth, then it can."

"What do you mean? How dangerous is it in this valley?" Morlithis asked.

Slarn set his meal down. "This is the Kiernane's region. They are a dangerous and vicious race and will not hesitate to kill you," Slarn replied.

"So don't hesitate to kill them," added Leo.

"They are savages and travel in packs. Though there are many factions, they do not like strangers in their land and will unite if threatened," Slarn continued.

"They wield weapons, but their clawed hands are a weapon of their own, even more deadly than our own claws. They use their maws, as well, in battle just as often as their weapons and claws," Leo continued.

"They are not skilled fighters," Slarn added. "But they always travel in packs, and because of their sheer numbers and fierceness, they are formidable."

"Their strength lies in their numbers, but their weakness is that they are sloppy fighters. If you find yourself in battle with them, it is best to fight one-on-one. They are easily defeated in small numbers," Leo said.

Morlithis nodded, and the four ate in silence after that, the atmosphere no longer feeling conducive to lighthearted conversation. When they finished their meal, they readied for bed, Leo taking the first watch at the mouth of the cave just to one side of the waterfall so he could see both the small opening to the side of the falls as well as beyond the water.

***

At dawn, Morlithis ended his watch by waking the rest of his counterparts, and they gathered their supplies, soon continuing in search of the catnip. Leo and Slarn had explained what to look for and the areas in which it grew in the valley. They traveled through the valley with no opposition, and though they could sense each other's

17

nervousness, they never voiced their concerns, and they each knew that they all could feel the eyes watching them.

A half day's journey found each of them on edge as they began hearing the faintest growling and cracking of twigs, and whenever one of their party startled, the rest instantly readied for an attack, but nothing came. When they heard nothing, it seemed even worse than hearing the cracking or growling. They kept their weapons up, and they didn't speak as they traveled deeper into the forest. They felt the eyes always on them. When they heard noises, they could feel the eyes glaring at them between the growling. When they heard silence, they felt the eyes staring. The day crept on, and they crept even deeper into the forest, scanning the forest floor for the catnip.

Finally, Morlithis spotted the fuzzy heart-shaped leaf that Leo and Slarn had described to him.

"Look!" he exclaimed, running over to the weed, forgetting in his excitement for finding the catnip about the danger lurking in his surroundings.

"Morlithis, wait!" hollered Slarn. It was too late. Morlithis had already made his way to the weed several yards from the rest of the group.

Suddenly, the valley around them erupted in a blur of gray motion and blood-curdling growls. A dozen Kiernane attacked Morlithis. Caught unprepared and off guard, he panicked, scrambling for his battle-axe behind his back and falling to his back as a dozen attackers barreled down on him.

The first of the Kiernane raised his battle-axe for a fatal blow, then fell backward with a knife sunk deep into his forehead. Morlithis saw a second knife down a second foe and two more felled by axes, and, taking advantage of the few seconds he now had, he quickly recovered, crawling to his knees and kneeling back against a tree beside him. Lightning fast, he unshouldered his crossbow and fired. Firing shot after shot, he reloaded arrow after arrow with blurring speed.

Leo, Fiera, and Slarn raced forward the moment the fierce enemy revealed themselves. Slarn had thrown his two long knives with precision, sending them deep into the skulls of the first two attacking Morlithis. Leo and Fiera didn't hesitate to fling an axe at the next two, downing them as well. Before their weapons hit their targets, they were already racing to retrieve them. Fiera and Leo still had their second axes, and Slarn, empty-handed, extended his claws—now his only weapon.

Both Leo and Fiera downed two more attackers easily with a quick parry and an axe to their respective attacker's leg. The two Kiernane fell to their backs, clutching their gushing stumps, their severed legs lying beside them.

Slarn had a more difficult time dispatching his next few foes but did so quickly. The first attacker opened himself up for an attack as he swung his battle-axe down at Slarn. Slarn sidestepped and tore a chunk out of his attacker's throat with his clawed fingertips. The attacker dropped his axe and stumbled backward, clutching his bleeding jugular, the blood pouring through his fingers.

His next foe was more cautious as he attacked, swinging with short, controlled slashes and keeping his guard up with his free arm or his axe. Slarn shuffled back, barely dodging the ferocious swings until his back found a tree. The attacker, seeing an opportunity, swung one last blow. Slarn dropped to his knees as the blade passed inches from his head and lodged deep into the tree with a thud. Slarn rolled as he slashed both his attackers' Achilles' heels. The Kiernane fell to the valley floor, and Slarn struck once more across his enemies' chests as he stood, slicing deep gashes in the creatures' them.

He saw an opening to retrieve his knives and darted toward the two dead foes that his blades now rested in. He then noticed half a dozen of the enemy pack advancing on Leo, who was busy holding his own with three Kiernane warriors.

"Morlithis!" Slarn hollered as he pointed at the half dozen Kiernane advancing on Leo and Fiera. Morlithis immediately understood and began firing arrow after arrow into the pack. Slarn dodged a sloppy attack from another enemy, rolled over the two corpses containing his knives, and yanked them free, dispatched his newest foe, then noticed Morlithis deflecting wild swings from three Kiernane warriors with his battle-axe. He was keeping his attackers at bay, but they were pushing him back. Slarn hurled his knives into the back of the heads of the first two, then turned around to see how Leo and Fiera were doing. They were also being pushed back.

"Morlithis, get the catnip!" Slarn ordered and darted toward several more of the enemy who were advancing on Leo from behind.

"Leo!" Slarn yelled as one of the Kiernane crept up behind Leo, bringing his axe down for a fatal blow. Leo spun around just in time to see the axe head descending. A black blur flashed across his vision. Then he was lying on his back. He heard Slarn scream, and then a pitch-black hand fell beside him.

"Slarn!" Leo yelled, scrambling back to his feet.

"Leo, get out of here!" Slarn yelled as he snatched up an axe with his good hand, holding his bleeding stump under his armpit, and ferociously pressed in on the Kiernane unlucky enough to be caught in his wake.

Slarn pressed forward, forcing the Kiernane away from Leo and Fiera with ferocity as more enemy warriors advanced on Slarn.

"Slarn!" Leo hollered as Fiera grabbed him by the shoulders.

"Leo!" Slarn yelled as he chopped down a foe. "Go!"

"Slarn!" Leo screamed as Slarn pushed the enemy forces even farther away.

Morlithis appeared by Leo's side with a handful of catnip then.

"I have the catnip!" he reported.

"Leo, we have what we came for. We need to leave!" Fiera said.

"No!" Leo replied.

"Leo, don't let his death be in vain!" Fiera nodded for Morlithis to leave. "Make your choice, but we need your help getting back," she said and then ran off after Morlithis.

Leo looked back at Slarn then at Fiera as she ran. Then back at Slarn. He finally darted off after Fiera. He would not let Slarn's death be for nothing. He would ensure

that Fiera and Morlithis would get the catnip back to save

the king if it was the last thing he did.

Chapter 3

Leorneth Led Morlithis and Fieraneth through the Yeshen Valley. They could hear behind them the vicious yearning growls for blood of the Kiernane as they hunted them.

They were beginning to tire, and Leo knew that they wouldn't be able to keep running much longer. The Kiernane had their scents now, so they knew they couldn't hide. Even if they did outrun them, it would only manage to delay the inevitable.

He knew there was only one way to lose these ferocious enemies. They had to mask their scents long enough to escape.

He frantically searched the forest floor for something that would be able to give them an advantage. A patch of mint or a dead carcass—anything that would throw off their scent.

His eyes darted back and forth as he ran, scanning the forest so fast that he almost missed them: a patch of mushrooms several yards away.

"Come on!" he ordered and darted toward the large mushroom patch.

The instant he came to the edge of the patch, Leo dropped to his knees and started grabbing mushrooms, smearing them on his leather armor and fur.

"Come on. We have to cover our scents. Squish as many as you can on you," he said.

The two didn't need Leo to explain. They had already followed suit, knowing that they needed to mask their scents.

They spent the next few seconds frantically squishing and rubbing the mushrooms all over their bodies, then dropped flat and started rolling and rubbing against the mushrooms, all the while inching their way farther into the center of the mushroom patch.

"Leo, look," Morlithis said and pointed to a small ditch just a few feet away.

Leo nodded, and the three crawled their way through the patch and took cover in the ditch.

The pack came into view then, just as they scrambled into the ditch. They poured into view like a title wave smashing against a wall as, one by one, they suddenly stopped and sniffed the air, smacking into each other as they skidded to a halt.

The three ducked behind the ditch and waited, ready to make their stand. Several of their enemies stepped closer, sniffing the air around them, and the three crouched lower. They heard the sniffs of the Kiernane. They heard the growls. They heard the steps closer, but they dared not look. Then they heard huffs and growls, followed by footsteps fading away into the forest.

They waited several moments, hearing more footsteps padding away, then returning. Hearing the guttural growls of the Kiernane as they moved about, growing louder, then softer to one side, then the other side. They still dared not move an inch, fearing that the slightest noise would reveal their location to the bloodthirsty hounds.

After what seemed like hours, they finally heard the last of their hunters give up. As quietly as he could, Leo slowly peeked his head out over the ditch. The pack had left.

Although the threat was gone, none of the three moved from their concealment for several more minutes until, finally, Leo cautiously stood to his feet, raising his battle-axes in preparation for battle.

He waited.

No attacks came, and he relaxed his grip.

Morlithis and Fiera both relaxed as they saw Leo release his axes.

"Looks like we are clear," Leo said. "But I don't know how long this will work. We will need to keep moving. They will surely be searching for us."

***

The three companions traveled without rest for the remainder of the day, and as dusk fell, they neared the waterfall, quickly spotting two dozen of the Kiernane standing guard around the entrance.

"How do they know about the entrance?" Leo asked.

"Leo, look." Fiera pointed to the left of the waterfall.

Leo's heart pounded in both excitement and horror as he saw his best friend lying on the ground, tied and beaten. His left wrist was wrapped in a dirty and bloodied cloth. His fur was matted and bloodied. Patches of fur had been yanked out and were now bloodied bald patches where the fur had once been. His face was swollen, and it appeared as though his eyes were bloated shut and his right ear was missing.

"Slarn's alive! We have to save him," Leo hollered and charged the enemy before Fiera or Morlithis could stop him.

"Come on!" she ordered and followed Leo. Morlithis quickly fell in behind her.

Leo rushed into battle, unsheathing his axes, and was upon his first two enemies in seconds. He downed them quickly, catching them off guard, and continued with a fierceness that unnerved even the Kiernane.

He brought swing after swing down on his next foe. The warrior frantically dodged swing after swing as Leo pressed in with no regard for his own safety, leaving opening after opening for a retaliating strike, but his enemy was too preoccupied with keeping Leo's axes at bay to attempt any attack.

**

Fiera and Morlithis each downed a foe of their own before the rest guarding the waterfall reached them.

**

"I'm coming, Slarn! I'm coming!" Leo yelled as he finally dispatched his foe, meeting head-on two more of his warriors, throwing an axe into the chest of one and charging full speed into the second.

Leo's axe barely came up in time to block his opponent's axe as he barreled into his attacker. The two tumbled to the ground. Only Leo returned to his feet.

**

Fiera and Morlithis fought through the dozen Kiernane. The only reason they survived was their skill with the blade, downing six attackers between parries and dodges, but they could not gain ground.

The last two of the six they downed were dispatched by mere luck as Morlithis tripped, avoiding a fatal blow, causing his enemy to lose balance, and knocking into one of the last four left.

Fiera took advantage of the clumsiness and brought her axes down upon the two Kiernane struggling to find their balance.

One of the Kiernane warriors was just about to dispatch Morlithis as he was easy prey, clumsily scrambling back to his feet, when one of the warriors guarding Slarn ordered a retreat, and their opponents fled.

***

Leo cut down the last of his opponents with the same careless abandon as he did the first four, but before he could reach Slarn, one of the Kiernane ordered a retreat, and the rest of the pack fled into the forest, the last dragging Slarn behind him.

"Nooo!" Leo screamed and chased after the five, only to be stopped by three who hid in the shadows of the trees. Leo cut them down swiftly, but not before the rest of the fleeing Kiernane disappeared into the brush.

"Leo!" Fiera yelled. "Wait!"

Leo looked back at her.

"He's gone. We will go after him, but you have to think with a clear head."

Leo nodded.

"Okay, we still need to get the catnip to the king before it's too late." Fiera looked at Morlithis. "Morlithis will take the catnip while we rescue Slarn."

Leo nodded in agreement.

"Okay, Morlithis, you start back. Be careful. There might be some of the Kiernane who have climbed up the cliff. We have no idea if any of them left the valley."

"Good luck," Morlithis said and began his trek back up the waterfall.

"Leo, I know you want to charge after Slarn, but we need to rest. We can't rescue Slarn if we are dead."

Leo stared at Fiera, who locked gazes with him defiantly. Finally, Leo strode past her to the cliff edge and plopped down, staring off into the forest. Fiera sat down beside him.

The two sat keeping a keen eye on the trees only yards away as they rested.. Fiera rummaged through her pack and handed Leo a tied-off food wrap. "Eat," she ordered.

Leo took the wrap frustratedly and yanked the tie off, then began tossing the small squares of cheese and bread into his mouth, staring into the fast-approaching night as Fiera found another food wrap and started eating as well. When they finished their food, Leo finally stood.

"We have rested enough," he said. Fiera didn't argue but stood to her feet. "Let's find Slarn," she said, and the two ventured into the dark forest.

It wasn't hard to track the pack dragging Slarn as they left a very profound path. They had been tracking Slarn's captors for half of the night when they happened upon a patch of mushrooms.

"Leo," Fiera said, pointing to the mushrooms. "We had better hide our scent again."

Leo nodded in agreement, and the two took the next few minutes squishing and wiping the mushrooms all over their armor and bare fur until it was matted down with the foul-smelling paste of the crushed fungus.

When they finally caught up with the pack, the two knew that they were close to the Kiernane village as they had passed several totems symbolizing warnings to venture no farther into the tribe's land.

Leo and Fiera crawled low, keeping to the tall grass and shrubbery, upwind from the pack.

The Kiernane were resting, it appeared, and eating. Slarn sat against a tree on the far side, bleeding, bruised, and swollen. His bandage around his nub was soaked in blood.

Leo burned with rage at the sight of his best friend so savagely beaten. He clenched his fists so tightly that he drew blood with his claws, growling a low guttural growl.

The Kiernane began sniffing the air, glancing around as they smelled the mushroom and blood.

Leo jumped to his feet, drawing his axes and throwing one after the other into the chests of the two nearest enemies, felling them as quickly as they'd leapt to attack him.Fiera leapt to her feet, throwing an axe into the chest of a third foe, and quickly dispatched her next opponent as Leo rushed the last members of the pack, his deadly claws slashing and slicing. Leo's first enemy was dead before he even hit the ground. The two finished off all the remaining Kiernane in similar brutal fashion, both scanning their surroundings for any signs of more foes before rushing to Slarn's side.

"Slarn, are you okay?" Leo asked. Slarn weakly smiled, his white teeth showing brightly in contrast to his midnight-black fur.

"Come on, let's get you home," Fiera said and untied Slarn's rope. The two helped him to his feet and began their trek back to the waterfall, yanking their weapons out of their dead enemies' corpses on the way.

Chapter 4

Morlithis climbed his way up the waterfall path. It was slow going, like it was on his way into the valley. He kept his eyes darting in all directions as he inched his way up the sloping path, keeping an eye out for any Kiernane.

Night fell fully, and he continued, not needing the daylight to see. Though colors dulled with his night vision, he could see almost just as well as if it were daylight.

He could see movement above, and he knew that there were indeed Kiernane on this path. He only hoped that they wouldn't be able to smell him. The mist had soaked his fur and had undoubtedly washed off the mushrooms by now, but he hoped that the stench of the squished fungi was still potent enough to cover his scent.

Morlithis had become used to the foul odor a long time ago and, as a result, had no idea if the mushrooms were still working or not.

He reached around his back, feeling for the hilt of his small battle-axe, and felt the wet, cold steel in his palm. At least he had his axe, he thought.

It wouldn't make much of a difference if he came across the Kiernane. He was confident that he could hold his own in battle, but if Leo and Slarn were right—and from his experience fighting them so far, they were—the Kiernane fought in packs, and he knew that he couldn't fend off an entire pack of these creatures. He only hoped that he could make it back to the safety of his people before the Kiernane found him. That, and he needed to somehow scale this cliff, climb back onto flat ground, and get past them all without being caught—and he had no idea how he was going to do it.

His bow had been broken during the initial fight with the Kiernane back in the valley. Now all he had was his small battle-axe.

He spent the rest of the climb continually glancing up toward the Kiernane above him. His hands were numb from the nighttime cold, and the mist that now soaked through his fur made him miserable in the cold of the night.

He was more than halfway up the zigzagging trail, and as he looked up toward the Kiernane above him, he could now see two. He was gaining on them, but it didn't appear that they had noticed him yet, so he waited until the two enemy warriors were beyond his vision.

He slowed his pace, ensuring that he wouldn't catch up to his foes before reaching the top of the waterfall. When Morlithis finally reached the cliff top, he slowly peeked his head over the edge, just enough to search the edge of the forest. He saw no signs of his enemy, but he knew if they had caught his scent, then it was likely that they were waiting in ambush for him.

He checked the pouch he had stuffed the catnip into and gripped the hilt of his battle-axe one more time, then he climbed up off the cliff and ventured into the night forest. He crept through the forest slowly at first, scanning for any hints that the Kiernane were nearby. The deafening roar of the waterfall drowned out all other sounds, and he felt vulnerable not being able to hear.

He wouldn't be able to hear the enemy trying to sneak up on him. He couldn't hear the crunching of leaves or the cracking of twigs, and that unnerved him.

His training had never prepared him for this, and he felt, now, wholly inadequate for a warrior of the Feleine.

With every scurrying critter that he saw or the sudden movement of branches, he froze, waiting for the Kiernane to attack.

He thought he heard growling behind him, and when he spun around, he thought he saw a form, but as he stared, he saw no more movement, even with his dark vision.

He turned back around and continued toward the Feleine borders, picking up his pace to a slow jog.

He didn't make it much farther before he started hearing the growling again. This time he knew that it wasn't his mind playing tricks on him, so he started running.

He didn't make it a hundred feet before the growls became louder and more threatening. He heard them all around him now, and he heard the cracking of twigs from all around him.

He ran faster, his heart pounding in his chest, and his breath came heavy as he ran at a full sprint now. He ran until his throat hurt and his nostrils flared with dryness. He could barely breathe, though he gulped in air like he had just come up from a long stint underwater. His chest hurt with every breath, and his legs felt more like rubber now than anything, and his hand was numb from gripping his small axe so tightly.

The growls sounded as if they were right on top of him, and he could hear tree branches slapping something behind him as he pushed through them.

He ignored the thousands of scratches and cuts from his careless barreling through the brush and branches. The scratches and cuts were the least of his worries as he fled through the forest. As he ran for his life.

He finally gained the nerve to glance toward the sound of his pursuers, both to his right and his left. To his left, he saw in the dulled colors of his night vision the gray furred silhouettes of two Kiernane only yards away as they pushed past tree branches, and when he looked to his right, fear engulfed him as he saw three more.

He didn't bother glancing behind him, as there was no doubt there was at least one more giving chase.

Six Kiernane warriors!

He wouldn't last a minute against six without his bow.

He looked over again at the three warriors to his right and noticed one staring at him as it ran. When it saw Morlithis look at him, it smiled, sending a shiver down Morlithis's spine.

They were taunting him. They were playing with him.

He was trained with the axe, but he knew that he couldn't defeat so many on his own. Morlithis panicked then, bringing his axe up as he rushed the taunting enemy, twisting around to swing a wild swing at his foe.

The Kiernane warrior responded with an attack of his own, knocking Mortlithis's axe out of his hand and slamming hard into the calico cat.

The two tumbled to the forest floor in a heap, and Morlithis felt the sting of his foe's deadly teeth sink into his unprotected shoulder where his cuirass did not cover.

Morlithis squirmed out of his enemy's grasp, ripping his shoulder from the maw of the vicious Kiernane, and the enemy warrior jumped to his feet as Morlithis scrambled to his, and the rest of the pack surrounded him.

Morlithis did the only thing that he could, then, without a weapon. He charged the recovering Kiernane again.

In an instant, the surrounding pack rushed Morlithis as the Kiernane warrior dodged and attacked Morlithis's reckless assault with a clawed hand slicing across the back of Morlithis's leather cuirass.

Morlithis's armor saved his life, but the Kiernane's attack sent the already panicked Feleine warrior into further panic, and he spun in mid-stride, swinging a clawed hand of his

47

own out wide in an attempt to slash a gash in his enemy's unarmored chest. However, as he spun around wildly, he caught a glimpse of the rest of the pack rushing in, distracting him from his attack, which fell short as he stumbled backward in terror. Morlithis fell to his back as a result of a sudden shift of the terrain into a descending slope, which sent him tumbling down a hillside with such dizzying speed that he could neither find a handhold to stop his roll nor steady himself enough to prevent him from falling off of the cliff rushing up at him.

Chapter 5

Leorneth, Slarnath, and Fieraneth didn't make much headway toward the waterfall before they heard the angry howls echoing through the night.

The three stopped, listening to the howls. There were just a few at first, not far off, then moments later more, fainter howls. Then even more. Over the next few moments, the howls filled the night as more and more Kiernane joined in until the three couldn't even make out when new howls began and when others stopped, then they trailed off into eerie silence.

"We need to pick up our pace," Leo said and turned to Slarn. "Can you go any faster?" Slarn stood straight, grimacing.

"If it means keeping ahead of those howls, I can." Leo nodded.

"Okay, first thing is covering our scents again. If we can make it to the mushroom patch, we might be able to rest a few minutes there."

"We'll have to change Slarn's bandage too," Fiera said.

49

Leo nodded. "Let's go."

***

Morlithis awoke and instantly felt the throbbing agony of the Kiernane bite at his shoulder. He felt as well the sharp stinging from the hundreds of cuts and scrapes beneath his sweat-soaked fur on his legs, arms, and even his face, though the pain paled in comparison to his shoulder.

He screamed from the sudden onslaught of pain pulsing throughout his body that instantly wrenched his mind out of the confusion and cloudiness that usually accompanied waking. Instead, his mind jolted to alertness, and he noticed that he was lying on a cold hard rock ledge that jutted out of the cliff he had just fallen over and overlooked the treetops. He lie flat on his stomach, staring out into the vast canyon forest before him that stretched out hundreds of yards, and he could just barely see the other side of the canyon cliffside with his night vision.

He knew the Yeshen Valley had no canyons, and he knew of only one canyon near his people's land: the Lithara

Canyon. If what he looked at now was the Lithara Canyon, then his journey home would indeed be dangerous.

Morlithis pushed himself up, hollering out again as he lifted himself, then clutched his wounded shoulder. He felt something warm, and when he withdrew his hand, he saw a bloodied palm. He noticed then, as well, the pool of blood on the ledge where he had been lying.

He was losing blood. He needed to dress his wound. His pack hadn't come loose during his battle, nor his fall, thankfully, and he was glad that he packed his medical kit in his pack. He shifted his weight and held back a scream as his shoulder erupted in fresh agony. With his good hand, he gently slid the pack strap off his wounded shoulder. Every movement and every touch sent another wave of pain through his arm, and it took his all not to cry out.

When the strap slid below his wound, he pulled the strap off his good shoulder, letting the pack plop to the ground. He grabbed the travel pack's strap with his good arm and slid it around onto his lap, trying not to move his injured shoulder.

51

Fresh surges of pain pulsed through his shoulder with every minuscule movement, and he fought the urge to scream out every time, forcing himself to focus on finding his medical kit in his pack.

He found it quickly, despite his slowness, and set it on the ground beside him, unstrapping the leather tie holding the rolled, bulky leather piece closed. It flopped open, revealing the half dozen tied pouches and a roll of cloth.

Morlithis untied the cloth and opened the pouch right next to the fabric with his good arm. He pulled out a vile that contained a green paste from the pocket and yanked the cork out with his teeth, then tossed his pack to the side with a gasp. Setting the vile on his lap, he unfolded the cloth strip, then snatched up the vile again and shook out its contents onto the center of the cloth.

The paste fell in a thick clump onto the cloth, and Morlithis carefully slid his palm under the fabric, holding the paste up, and took a deep breath, knowing what was to come.

He let out a long breath and smashed the paste-filled cloth onto his wounded shoulder, howling in pain and leaning back against the cliff wall.

He whimpered and closed his eyes, forcing his mind away from the pain, then he felt the paste working as he pressed his hand against his wounded shoulder.

The paste had started numbing the bite wound, and he could feel the tingle of the healing properties of the paste working where the numbness hadn't begun working fully. The pain lessened, and he opened his eyes, reveling in the relief a moment as he looked over the canyon. He started gently wrapping the cloth around his shoulder, wrapping the length of the strip around his shoulder a couple of times, then unstrapped his cuirass. The medicine had started working even more, numbing the pain enough and allowing him to move his shoulder freely with only a heavy throbbing. He knew the medication wouldn't fully numb the pain, but it would allow him to move without excruciating agony, and that was enough.

Once the cuirass was off, he wrapped the cloth across his chest to secure the bandage in place, wrapping the last of the strip back around his back under his armpit and around his shoulder one last time, and tied it off under his arm.

When he was satisfied that the bandage was secure, he donned his cuirass, noticing the leather armor's scratches. It had indeed saved his life; even where the Kiernane had bitten him, he could see teeth marks at the edge of the shoulder, and he knew that if he had not been wearing it, he would surely be dead.

***

Leo, Slarn, and Fiera reached the mushroom patch soon after the howling stopped and squished mushrooms all over their fur and armor, then shoved more into their packs for later use.

When they finished, they rested for a few minutes and redressed Slarn's nub, applying healing paste from Leo's medical kit, and then continued their journey.

They were exhausted, but they knew that they couldn't stop for long, not while they were being hunted, and not while they were in this valley so close to their mortal enemy.

Slarn's injuries, though now not as severe as before due to the healing salve they applied, were slowing the group down, and they all knew it was just a matter of time before the Kiernane found them, even with the mushrooms masking their scents.

They were finally nearing the waterfall when Fiera pulled on Leo's arm, pointing to Kiernane footprints.

Leo spotted the tracks almost immediately, and the three followed the Kiernane footprints, discovering several more sets and even more footprints meeting up with the ones they were tracking.

When the three grew closer, following the footprints to the waterfall, they could hear the subtle rumble of a small encampment, and when they reached the tree line, their suspicions were indeed confirmed when they saw the small army at the base of the waterfall.

"There is no way we'll be able to fight past that many," Fiera said as the three crouched behind a thick bush.

"We will have to take the long way around," Leo replied.

"That will add another two days," Fiera said.

"Three at our current pace." Leo turned to Slarn. "Can you make the journey?" he asked.

"Do I have a choice?"

"No, I guess not."

They noticed several of the Kiernane start sniffing the air.

"It's time for us to go, quickly," Leo ordered, and the three disappeared back into the dense forest.

The three traveled as fast as they could for as far as they could before resting under a tree with thick and full low-hanging branches, surrounded by heavy brush.

"We will rest here only a short while," Leo said. "We can set camp when we get farther from Kiernane territory. We must try to reach the pass of Criental before we stop again. There, it will be safer to camp."

Slarn and Fiera nodded in agreement, and soon the three were heading for the pass.

They traveled through the rest of the night and into the morning before they reached the pass, and when they finally came to it, they set up camp on a ridge at the mouth of the pass, which allowed them to see in both directions amongst the heavy brush.

Leo remembered the pass from his days in the war before they had made the secret waterfall trail. He had camped many times in the pass with the army. It was the perfect encampment for a sizable army. The steep, treeless slopes on either side made it impossible for anyone to sneak up on them, let alone traverse it. If there were lookouts posted at the tree line, there was no chance of a surprise attack from those who might safely find a way down.

It was the mouth of the pass that needed the attention. With an entire army at one's disposal, simple guard posts and lookouts were warning enough. However, with the three of them, they needed a much more secure camp, so they camped on the ridge.

They were somewhat concealed under a large tree atop the ridge, and the slope of the hill was clear of trees, so that allowed for a clear line of sight for at least a few yards. It was enough of a warning to wake the others up if any Kiernane attacked, and they didn't have to worry about bowmen because the Kiernane never used bows. They liked to see their victims up close as they killed them, the savages that they were.

"Slarn, you rest while Fiera and I set up camp," Leo ordered.

Slarn would have objected at not pulling his own weight setting up camp, but he doubted he would be much use anyway. He was exhausted—more than he should have been—and although the healing salve was doing its job of numbing the pain, it only numbed so much.

Slarn didn't argue, and he was asleep in minutes.

"I'll stay here and keep watch over Slarn while you forage for food," Leo said. "There should be plenty of food in the pass to fill us, but stay alert, just in case."

Fiera nodded and made her way down the ridge in search of food, returning minutes later, cradling an armful of various fruits.

"You weren't kidding about having plenty of food," she said as she neared, dropping them onto the ground.

Leo smiled as he snatched a fruit from the pile and woke Slarn up.

"Here, Slarn, eat. You need energy."

Slarn groggily opened his eyes and sluggishly grabbed the round green fruit.

The three ate their fill, then Leo volunteered to take the first watch, allowing both Fiera and Slarn to sleep, waking Fiera several hours later for her watch, and soon falling asleep himself.

Fiera had been on watch only a few hours when she saw six Kiernane warriors step out into the open and howl.

She didn't need to wake Leo or Slarn, as the howling did that for her.

Leo jumped to his feet, unsheathing his battle-axes as Slarn sluggishly stood.

"Stay behind us, Slarn, you are in no condition to fight," Leo ordered.

The Kiernane rushed up the ridge with their own axes drawn and their vicious growls leading their charge.

Chapter six

Morlithis moved his arm in circles, testing the freshly applied healing salve as he stood to his feet. The ointment had only been applied minutes before and was already working. His shoulder ached, but that was about it now. It felt less like he had been wounded and more like soreness from a long day of bow practice.

After donning his cuirass, he tied his medical kit back into a roll and tossed it into his pack, then took a few minutes to eat one of his travel rations. He thought about home then and remembered the catnip, bringing both hands to the pouch at his belt in fright. It was still there. It hadn't fallen off during the battle—if you could call it that—with the Kiernane or his fall.

Luck had indeed been with him, and he would need that luck if he were to make his way through the Lithara Canyon.

He craned his neck, looking up toward the cliff top, searching for a way to climb back up, then looked carefully over the ledge, looking down toward the canyon floor, searching for a way down. It appeared equally tricky and dangerous in either direction.

Finally, he chose the Lithara Canyon, but first, he would rest and wait until daylight to find a way down. He feared traveling the Lithara Canyon at night, especially injured and tired as he was, so he laid down against the cliff wall and slept, using his pack as a pillow.

***

Morlithis woke to the blinding rays assaulting his eyes as the sun rose above the canyon's far cliff wall. The harsh, blinding light gave him no mercy as he opened his eyes, only to close them again. He shifted his weight, and he was reminded of his wounded shoulder. He inspected his bandages, though he knew he wouldn't be able to do anything about them if they were too dirty, anyway.

He moved his shoulder around, testing the healing paste. It was still working, and his shoulder felt little more than sore, at least for now, and he readied himself for the undoubtedly painful climb down the cliff.

After he donned his pack, secured his catnip pouch, and tested his arm again, he laid over the ledge, searching for hand- and footholds.

After a few moments, he finally took a long, hard breath and spun his legs around, dangling them over the edge of the ledge, his foot searching for the first of the footholds. Once he secured his foot on a jutting piece of rock, he slid the rest of his body over the edge, gripping the ledge so tightly that his fingers lost circulation.

He searched for the next piece of jutting rock to use as a foothold. He found one just a couple inches from the other and stretched his free foot over to it. When he was satisfied that he had a good hold of it, he reached a hand over to the nearest jutting rock to use as a handhold. Once he had a secure grip on the handhold, he found another handhold for his free hand.

He continued this process repeatedly, slowly making his way down the cliffside. He made it only a quarter of the way down before fatigue began to overtake him, and he had been down-climbing for hours. Progress had been slow and tiring, and he knew that he would not make it down before his body gave out.

His mouth was dry, but he dared not even try to reach for water. He hadn't even thought to take it out of his pack, and he knew that trying to fish it out now would literally kill him. His shoulder was throbbing unbearably now, not because the salve wasn't working, but because of the use of his injured shoulder. He could only imagine what it would be like if he didn't have any healing paste on it.

He had an idea, though it was dangerous and foolish to attempt; he didn't see any other way, and he knew he couldn't keep climbing down at such a snail's pace. One could argue that it wasn't any more foolish an idea than trying to climb down off a cliff with no water.

He was below the treetops now, and so he thought that he might be able to find a branch close enough to jump to. He carefully turned his neck as far behind him as he could without moving the rest of his body and saw a branch out of the corner of his eye, so he turned his head the other way for a better view. He turned too fast, dizzying himself, and he lost his grip on the single, tiny protruding handhold on the side of the rock face that both hands were clinging to.

He felt his sweaty, furry hands slip off the little grip, and he began to fall backward. He frantically reached for the grip again, feeling his fingertips scrape against the grip as he tried to take hold of the rock, but still, he continued backward.

He did the only thing that he could think of then. He pushed off the cliff wall with all his strength, launching himself toward the tree branch.

A moment later, he felt the leaves brush his hands as he plummeted to the canyon floor.

**

Leorneth and Fieraneth stood their ground as the Kiernane pack charged at them, and Slarnath stood weakly behind, weaponless. His only defense: his extended claws from his one good hand.

Leo charged down the hill as the first two warriors neared him, and he dropped to his knees between them as they

65

swung their axes out wide. Using his momentum to slide between his two enemies, he severed their inside legs at the knees.

The two creatures fell to the ground in howls of pain, clutching their gushing wounds as Leo used one of his axe blades to stop his slide and jump back to his feet just in time to dodge an almost fatal attack from another enemy warrior.

***

Fiera waited for the first of her opponents to attack, dodging the wild swing easily, bringing a foot into the warrior's chest, and sending him backward, stumbling into a second Kiernane warrior behind him. Both tumbled down the steep slope.

The last of the attacking warriors dodged his two falling counterparts and lunged at Fiera with a wild swing of his own. Fiera brought an axe up, knocking the deadly weapon aside as she sidestepped and brought her second axe up into the chest of her opponent.

The creature gurgled a muffled howl as it fell to the ground with Fiera's axe still deep in his chest. Fiera didn't bother retrieving her axe as the first two Kiernane warriors regained their footing and charged her ferociously.

***

Leo retaliated with a fatal blow of his own as the Kiernane warrior yanked his axe head out of the soft ground, barely freeing the axe before he fell dead.

***

Fiernath again waited for her two opponents to near and focused all her energy on pressing her attack when they reached her.

She swung her axe with the strength of both hands now, with rocking force, and she slammed her blade into her enemy's axe with a loud clang, forcing the weapon down. In a flash, she brought an elbow to the neck of the warrior as she spun into her second attacker's attack and brought her axe up barely in time to block the deadly swing with such force that she knocked the Kiernane warrior off balance, and he tumbled down the hill.

She quickly dispatched the recovering warrior left beside her as Leo stepped up to her side.

The Kiernane warrior finally stopped tumbling down the hillside, jumping to his feet with a defiant howl, and disappeared back into the forest.

"We need to go," Leo ordered, turning around to Slarn. "We are leaving. They will be back and with a much larger force. We need to get as far into this pass as we can before they get back," he said, marching back up the hill.

Slarn nodded, and the three headed into the pass, Leo and Fiera snatching up their packs.

Chapter seven

Leo led Slarn and Fiera through the pass as quickly as Slarn could walk. They heard the howling replies of the Kiernane warriors already. They were still far off, but they each knew that would change quickly.

"The pass is overgrown with mushrooms. That is why we used this as a camp during the war," Leo told Fiera. "We will stop then for a short rest and to collect as many mushrooms as we can. We will have a long few days ahead of us, and we will need them if the Kiernane pursue us past the pass," he finished.

A few minutes' walk farther, the forest floor looked as if it had more mushrooms than trees or grass. Mushrooms had even grown onto the base of the trees, and the sweet smell of the fungi wafted through the air powerfully, filling their nostrils with their unique sweet scent with a hint of a foul odor that resembled the stench of rot or soured food. Though the stench was barely noticeable in small patches, it was unmistakable now that they were in the pass. It was why the Kiernane had such difficulty tracking anyone who smothered the fungus on them.

"You will get used to the smell," Leo said, seeing Fiera's face twist in disgust. Leo turned to Slarn. "We will rest when we get farther into the patch," Leo said, and Slarn nodded.

A few minutes later, Leo spoke up again. "We will rest here. We can afford only a few minutes, and then we must keep going." Fiera and Slarn nodded, and the three each found a tree to sit against. They heard more howling again. This time it was much closer.

"They are getting closer," Fiera said.

"Yes. We will need to find somewhere to hide soon. I know of a cave that might keep us hidden for a while."

"Caves have cave dwellers," Slarn replied, "and if it is the cave that I think you are speaking of, we may not be much safer in there than out here."

"At least in there it will be only one creature. Besides, the beast sleeps during the day," Leo replied.

"Should we wake it, we may not fair well," Slarn replied.

"Then we must not wake it," Leo said.

Slarn nodded and laid his head against the tree, understanding that Leo had made up his mind and there was no changing it. "We shall not wake the beast, then," he said quietly and closed his eyes.

The three sat silently after their discussion until Leo started snatching up nearby mushrooms. Fiera soon followed suit, allowing Slarn to sleep. He did not have a pack anyway, and if he were to heal, he would need as much rest as he could get whenever he could find it.

They had rested longer than Leo had intended, but Slarn had been fast asleep, and Leo did not want to wake him. Though they couldn't spare the extra time, they could not afford to have Slarn get worse. They decided to continue through the pass when they heard more howling. The howling woke Slarn, who did not complain when Leo suggested they move quickly.

Slarn set the pace for the group, being the slowest member due to his injuries, but they still moved swiftly. More and more howls sounded as the three rushed through the thick forest pass, and with each round of howling, they sounded closer than the last. The Kiernane were on the hunt and moving at a much swifter pace than them.

"We have to hurry, Slarn!" Leo said. "The cave isn't much farther. You must go faster!"

Slarn pushed himself then, too hard, racing through the forest for mere minutes before he collapsed. Leo, who was right behind him, almost fell himself, stopping so abruptly at seeing his closest friend fall. Fiera, right behind Leorneth, had to shuffle to the side to keep from slamming into him as he halted.

"Is he okay?" she asked as Leo knelt beside Slarn.

"He is breathing, but his fur is soaked; even for running like we were, it is too wet. He is not doing well. Come on, help me." Leo hefted Slarn up, and Fiera rushed to Slarn's other side. They wrapped Slarn's arms around behind their necks and stood.

More howls erupted behind them, and they could tell the Kiernane were not far off.

"Come on. The cave isn't far," Leo said, and the two half-carried, half-dragged Slarn to the cave.

As Leo indicated, it was only a few dozen yards until they saw the cave. It was almost invisible in the tall brush and trees, and if one weren't looking for it, they could easily pass right by it, never even knowing the cave was there. Leo hoped that the Kiernane would just pass right by it.

The cave was elevated several feet off the ground, where the steep hillside turned into a cliff for a few yards before morphing back into the steep grassy hillside.

Leo nodded his head toward the cliff, directing Fiera toward it, then, as they neared the cave, Fiera jumped up to the entrance and, after a glance into the mouth of the cave, spun around.

Leo was already maneuvering Slarn into position so that Fiera could pull him up, and the two lifted their bulky and heavy friend onto the ledge, then Leo climbed up, and they dragged

Slarn into the darkness. Their dark vision took over as they entered the blackness of the cave, and the two waited. Waited for Slarn to wake and waited for the pending horde of Kiernane warriors to pass by—or find them.

***

Morlithis twisted his body as he fell, stretching for the next branch, and the next, and the next, desperately trying to grab hold of the branches flying past him. The ground jumped up toward him, and his heart pounded in his chest. Panic gripped him yet again, and he clawed at the thick branches rushing by. They sliced through his thick coat, scraping at his arms, but he ignored the stinging cuts. All he cared about was stopping his fall.

Finally, he found a grip and held on for dear life, but the branch bowed and snaped as Morlithis held on to it with all his strength. It did slow him momentarily, but when the branch snapped, Morlithis's downward momentum sent him flipping head over heels as he fell.

He felt the sting of the branches slapping at his legs, then his arms and face, then his legs again, then arms and face again. All the while, he tried frantically to catch hold of another branch well enough to slow his fall.

Again, he caught another branch. This time it was thicker and bore his weight better, slowing his fall almost to a stop before it snapped. Morlithis felt every branch smack, scratch, and punch as he tumbled through the thicker branches. One knocked the breath out of him as he fell right on it before it too snapped.

Branch after branch smacked, scratched, or punched him with no reprieve. He no longer flipped through the air, but each branch, now large enough to hold his weight, knocked him aside and into another lower branch as he fell until he finally landed with a painful jar onto the canyon floor.

Still recovering from the branch that gave him a gut punch, knocking the wind out of him, he didn't move, unable to breathe. When he finally found his breath again, he still didn't move. Every inch of his body hurt, and he could already feel the bruises forming beneath his fur.

***

The dark cave gave the three shelter from the Kiernane, but it came with its own dangers, and Leo kept staring deep into the darkness. The Kiernane had reached them only minutes after the three climbed into the cave, and there were dozens searching the pass for them. The fact that the pass was littered with mushrooms meant that the Kiernane couldn't track them anyway, but Leo and Fiera had still smeared several mushrooms over Slarn and themselves. It would be a different story when they had to leave the cave, though. The Kiernane might just find them anyway, due to the sheer number that were hunting them.

The three sat half a dozen yards into the cave, just far enough so that they could not be seen unless the Kiernane found the cave and climbed up into the entrance. Leo continued to glance back into the depths of the cave. It unnerved him to be so close to the beast of the pass, but as long as they left before it woke, they would be in no danger. This creature was easily

76

angered, but if it was left alone, no harm would come to them, that is unless it saw them in its home. During the war, the beast had made itself known but never attacked unless provoked, it killed only those handful of warriors who made the mistake of entering the cave at night when it was awake.

"How long are we going to stay here?" Fiera asked.

Leo snapped his neck around to glare at her menacingly.

"Keep quiet," he whispered harshly.

A low half gurgle, half growl echoed through the cave, and Leo snapped his head back toward the darkness, reaching for the hilt of an axe.

The two stared into the depths of the cavern's blackness, straining their dark vision to see any signs of movement. Finally, after several long seconds, Leo turned to Fiera and whispered, "We must leave before nightfall."

Fiera nodded and sat back, her gaze toward the darkness of the cave.

***

Morlithis slowly stood to his feet with a groan. His shoulder throbbed excruciatingly, and the rest of his body ached. It hurt to move even an inch, but he knew that he couldn't stay where he was.

He checked the catnip pouch on his belt and inspected his pack, tossing the catnip into it, realizing that the pouch would be safer in his pack rather than on his belt. He snatched up a thick branch as he began his trek, ripping off the protruding twigs and stomping on the end, breaking it into a point so that he had a makeshift spear.

He had a small knife in his pack and spare bowstrings for his bow, so he had the material to make a new bow, but that took time, and right now he just wanted to start home. Besides, he would need to make new arrows as well, and he didn't have any materials to make those just yet. So he would have to find the right items to make arrows on his way home.

Chapter eight

Although Morlithis had been traveling without so much as seeing more than scurrying critters, he had begun feeling uneasy shortly after starting his trek. He scanned the forest frequently and listened intently for any indications of danger. Every so often, he swore that he heard someone behind him, but never found any signs of pursuers. Still, he constantly felt like someone, or something, was watching him.

He held his makeshift spear that doubled as his walking stick, and the gash on the back of his hand trickled blood. He hadn't noticed it at first when he fell through the trees earlier that day, but he soon realized how deep of a cut he received. That wasn't the only gash the tree had given him, but it was the most severe, and he kept reopening the wound every time he tightened his grip on his spear. Every time something startled him.

He stopped to rest, pulling off his pack and pulling out his waterskin as he sat against a nearby tree. He sat only a few minutes drinking his water and was just about to search in his bag for the last of his food rations when he heard a low growl, and the hair on the back of his neck stood straight up.

He saw a pair of wolves emerge from the shadows. Then two more stalked their way out from his flank.

Morlithis froze as the four beasts showed themselves. His makeshift spear lay next to him, but he knew he wouldn't be able to grab it before the wolves reached him. Besides that, there were four of them. The wolves bared their teeth, then it all happened so fast that Morlithis didn't think, he just reacted.

Almost in unison, the four beasts attacked. Morlithis threw his pack toward the first pair as he rolled toward his spear. The pack smacked hard into one of the two wolves, sending it tumbling with the pack as the second wolf smashed its head hard against the tree Morlithis had been leaning against. Morlithis continued his roll as he grabbed his makeshift spear, bringing it up with the point toward the deadly beasts on his flank, which had also lunged at him. The first impaled itself on the spear with a loud yelp as Morlithis brought the spear up without a second to spare. The second wolf landed on top of Morlithis, pinning him to the ground as it snapped its head down for a bite out of Morlithis's jugular. Luckily, the dying wolf's weight at the end of his spear shifted his weapon as the wolf pinned him so that the wolf found the wood of his spear instead of the flesh of Morlithis's neck.

Morlithis struggled desperately to free himself as the creature took only seconds to snap the spear in half. In doing so, the creature shifted its weight on Morlithis, allowing him to shove the wild beast off him. The wolf cut short a yelp and fell limp at his side, the broken spear protruding from the creature's neck.

Morlithis didn't have time to wonder how he impaled the creature as the last two wolves recovered from their first attack, the first shaking the shock from its head at slamming into the tree, and the other untangling itself from Morlithis's pack.

Morlithis barely had time to yank the bloody half spear from his dead foe next to him and bring it up into the stomach of one of the two wolves. Morlithis shoved the dying wolf into the other with all his might as it fell onto the skewer. The wild beast's weight helped Morlithis alter the limp creature's trajectory, as he only needed to move the spear mere inches, and the dog's own weight pulled it to the side, crashing into its counterpart. The last wolf yelped in surprise as it fell to the side of Morlithis. Morlithis didn't hesitate. He scrambled to his feet, darting for the first wolf he killed as the last wolf crawled its way free from the corpse on top of it.

Morlithis practically fell to the ground, scrambling for the spear as the beast raced after him. Morlithis yanked the broken spear free from the wolf corpse just as the last wolf sprang for him. Morlithis didn't give the creature a chance to finish its attack, jabbing the broken spear into the wolf's side as the beast brought its maw down on Morlithis's side, then the wolf went limp without even a yelp, its muzzle still clinging to Morlithis's cuirass. He could feel the teeth pressing against him, but he knew the bite had not penetrated his armor, and Morlithis was thankful once again for his armor. It had saved his life twice now in as many days.

Morlithis lay there, the wolf to his side, its jaw still clutching him, and scanned the forest for any signs of any more wolves. Once he was satisfied that there were no more wolves, he peeled the dead animal's muzzle off him, yanked the broken spear out of the dog, and climbed to his feet. He snatched up his pack, inspecting the damage it received from the beast and, finding only minimal damage, he slid it on, then scanned the forest again. Still nothing. He glanced at the four dead wolves and decided to save his rations and have a warm meal instead.

Morlithis made a small fire, cutting off several slabs of meat from one of the wolves, cooking them using one of the broken ends of his spear. He didn't take long to eat and frequently searched his surroundings for signs of a threat as he sat leaning against a tree. After less than a half hour, he was back up and on his way toward home again.

***

The day was nearing its end, and Morlithis was getting tired. His cuts and scrapes stung, and his shoulder throbbed. He held a piece of his broken spear in each hand now.

83

He heard voices nearby and froze, straining his ears to make out what they were saying. After a few moments, he realized that they were speaking Litharian. Though he had never heard it before, it was unmistakable, with its signature "s" sounds in almost every word and hissing sounds throughout the conversations.

He heard heavy footsteps approaching fast, snapping twigs and crunching leaves, and he took cover in a grouping of thick brush, ignoring the itching scrapes from the thorns.

A half dozen Lithar passed by, just seconds after he took cover, running toward the voices. Morlithis had never seen a Lithar before, though he had heard stories about their race when he traveled to the trading villages near the western outskirts of their land.

The Lithar were primitive, green-skinned lizard people with thick scalelike skin and powerful tails that they often attached spikes to the end of to use as another weapon in addition to their spiked clubs, and they had lizard-like snouts with teeth to rival that of the Kiernane.

Though Morlithis couldn't see the teeth of those running by, the rest of the descriptions he had heard were relatively accurate. These Lithar did indeed wield spiked clubs and spikes on their tails. They were smaller than the tales made them out to be, but still, he needed to keep clear of them if the stories were true.

He waited a few more seconds to make sure that no more were coming, and then as quietly as he could, he continued on his way, straining his ears for any more voices or footsteps.

He didn't make it far before running right into a smaller band of three Lithar, who immediately raised their clubs and hissed. Morlithis sprinted away, and they gave chase, but not before shouting warnings to their counterparts in Litharian. Morlithis didn't need to know what was said. His imagination answered that for him as he heard the hissing replies of more Lithar.

He ran—again—as he did before. He could hear more and more Lithar join the trio in giving chase, but he dared not look back.

He could stop and fight. Part of him wanted to, but a part of him wanted to flee. Besides, if he did stop and fight, like with the Kiernane, he wouldn't last long by himself, and he needed to get the catnip back to the priest-king.

That is what he told himself why he ran.

He knew that he should never have joined Leo and the others on this quest. He would fail, he knew. He would run because he was a coward. He would fight to the very end, if fleeing failed, but in the end, he knew that he would eventually fail.

Again, he hadn't run long before he came across another three Lithar. Morlithis skidded to a halt as the three stared at him, their deadly spears pointing out menacingly.

He fell backward, slipping on a twig, or leaf, or just the grass. He wasn't sure what he slid on, but it saved his life. He fell just as the massive Lithar before him lunged toward him, aiming his spear at Morlithis with his spear. The spear sunk deep into the neck of one of the Lithar chasing him.

Morlithis rolled, scrambling to flee as the unusually large Lithar advanced. He caught a glimpse of the other two Lithar, noticing that they too had skewered a couple of his pursuers also. Then one shouted a war cry like the cries of the other Lithar. Something about this one's voice was different than those chasing him. He realized then too that these new Lithar had gray skin instead of green, and they stood a good chest-high taller than the smaller green Lithar.

Dozens of the smaller green Lithar rushed in from the cover of the brush and trees around them, all attacking the three gray Lithar and ignoring him. The green Lithar slammed their spiked clubs into the legs and sides of the larger gray ones, who retaliated with jabs and swings of their own.

The green Lithar easily dodged most swings and stabs, but every few swings hit their mark, sending a green Lithar flying to smack hard into a tree and fall limp, or the pointy end of the larger Lithar's spikes sank into the necks of the smaller lizard-like creatures.

Two more of the larger gray Lithar rushed into battle from the trees beyond, plowing through a grouping of the green Lithar with ease as they swung their spears to and fro, knocking a half dozen of their foes into nearby trees or tumbling across the forest floor.

Morlithis scrambled to his feet as he saw more and more of the green Lithar pouring in, overwhelming the five. Then he saw a sixth, and a seventh, and an eighth of the larger gray Lithar enter the battle, and before he knew it, Morlithis was battling several of the green Lithar himself.

He swung with one of the broken halves of his spear and stabbed with the other, barely keeping them at bay as they swung and lunged at him. Suddenly an arrow sunk into the eye socket of one of his attackers, then another sunk into the neck of a second foe, and a third into the chest of yet another.

Then something sharp and powerful smacked into his back, and he went tumbling. When he finally finished rolling, he pushed himself off of the ground to see a thick green tail with spikes at its end flying toward him. He scrambled from the path of the spikes, but he was not fast enough to avoid the powerful tail altogether, and it sent him sprawling into a nearby tree. He hit with a loud crack, and everything went black.

Chapter nine

Leo gently shook Slarn awake.

"It is time to leave, my friend," he said as he saw Slarnath open his eyes.

"How are you feeling?" Fiera asked.

"Better," Slarn replied.

Leo and Fiera had re-bandaged his wrist and applied more of the healing paste shortly after entering the cave as he slept, waking Slarn in the process, so Leo gave him a health elixir to help his fever and sickness. It had worked to bring him out of his condition for the time being, but if he didn't get proper healing treatment, it would not keep.

Slarn stood to his feet, keeping his bandaged arm at his chest while pushing up with his good hand.

"I feel much better," he reported.

"Good, my friend. I wish we could give you more time to rest and heal, but it is dusk," Leo said.

They heard a low growling and sniffling from farther inside the cave, and all turned to stare down into the blackness.

"I see," Slarn said. "We should go, then."

Leo nodded and snatched up his pack, helping Slarn to his feet. Fiera followed, snatching her pack as well. Then they heard the roar of the beast as it fully woke, and the three ran to the mouth of the cave, jumping off the ledge and hurrying away.

They didn't get more than a few feet before a half dozen Kiernane warriors found them. The three halted in mid-step as the warriors intercepted them with their axes raised.

Slarn backed away, extending the claws from his one good hand as two Kiernane advanced, swinging their deadly axes for his head. Luckily for Slarn, the Kiernane were not tactical thinkers, and Slarn easily dodged the first axe with a duck as he backed toward a tree. The axe blade dug deep into the tree trunk with a thud, giving Slarn the time he needed to dodge the second Kiernane swing as his first opponent yanked his blade free of the tree.

Slarn dropped to his knees and slashed his claws across his new attacker's thigh, then rolled as the Kiernane warrior finally yanked his axe free and brought it down in a deadly arc.

The Kiernane's blade sank deep into his counterpart's stomach as the creature bent low to clutch his thigh.

***

Fiera unsheathed her axes just in time to block the powerful and wild swings of her opponents. One after the other, she could barely keep up with the attacks as they pressed in, pushing her farther and farther away from Leo and Slarn.

She finally saw an opening and took it. One of the warriors overextended his swing, knocking himself off balance ever so slightly, and he released one hand from his axe as he swung his blade out wide to steady himself. Fiera leapt in at that moment, ignoring the attack from her other adversary as she stepped toward the clumsy warrior, bringing both of her axes around for her attack. She felt the wind on her cheek from the blade that she ignored as she half-ducked sideways, lowering her shoulders so that she had a straight swing into the open side of her enemy's abdomen. Her blades sank into the furry flesh of the warrior, and she quickly yanked them free, ripping out chunks of flesh in the process.

The creature howled in pain and dropped to the forest floor as Fiera spun, bringing her axes back up, ready to defend attacks from her first foe as she straightened back up.

***

Leo sidestepped a deadly downswing that would have split his skull in half if he hadn't moved so quickly, dodging the blade and unsheathing his axes. Both Kiernane warriors attacked him with a fury that gave him little chance to recover at first, but within a few swings, Leo was able to get the advantage and chopped off the leg of the first of his opponents. The second warrior proved to be more difficult, and before Leo could dispatch him, two more Kiernane emerged from the brush, pushing him back and forcing him into a frenzy of parries and dodges.

***

Another half dozen Kiernane found their way to the battle and split their forces between the three and were just about to overwhelm the Feleine trio when the beast emerged with a fury out of the cave, lunging from the ledge into the forest floor and turning toward Leo, Fiera, and Slarn, still in the heat of battle. The creature roared defiantly, recognizing their scents, and charged. It was a creature unlike anything they had anywhere else in the valley or the Feleine lands. A very distant cousin to a bear, it was at least as large, and its six legs made it unbelievably fast. Its twin tails with poison barbs that dripped toxin when the creature became angry added a measure of horror to its ferocity. Its short green and brown striped fur lent another measure of terror as the beast easily disappeared into its forest surroundings. Its head was identical to a bear's except that it had a pair of tusks in the center of its mouth amid its deadly teeth.

Both Feleine and Kiernane alike stopped battling to turn and discover the beast racing toward them.

Luckily for the three Feleine creatures, the Kiernane jumped into action, attacking the creature. The beast destroyed its attackers in seconds as more Kiernane advanced, ignoring the three of them.

"Run!" Leo ordered. Neither Fiera nor Slarn questioned him, and the three ran.

***

"Leo! Stop!" Fiera hollered as she spun around, seeing Slarn once again collapsed. Leo stopped and turned as well, about to scold the two for wanting to stop when he saw why Fiera was so adamant. He rushed back over to Slarn and Fiera. Slarn had not passed out but lay flat on his stomach, gasping for air, and Fiera plopped down beside him upon noticing that he was not injured. Leo sat as well.

"We will rest for a few minutes, but we must keep going soon," Leo said.

Slarn ignored Leo, and Fiera nodded, and after a couple of minutes, when Fiera had caught her breath enough to talk, she said, "That beast was terrifying, and it killed those Kiernane like they were nothing."

"Yes," Leo replied, "it is a creature you never want to anger. Luckily it does not hold a grudge long. Good for us that the Kiernane had not known how dangerous it was."

"Yeah. Good for us," Fiera replied. "Do you think they killed it?"

"It depends on how many fought it. I suppose a few dozen might have been able to kill it. Hopefully it put up a good fight and killed most of them," Leo answered.

"Hopefully," Fiera said.

Slarn rolled over onto his back. "Want to go back and find out?" he asked with a grin.

"You are ready to keep going, I see," Leo said, ignoring his comment.

"I am ready."

"Let's go, then," Leo ordered.

***

The three traveled through the rest of the night without meeting a single Kiernane, and after a short conversation, they all agreed to keep traveling through the day, cutting their journey through the pass shorter by almost a full day. The pass had begun to slope upward shortly after they decided to continue, and the mushrooms gradually diminished until they disappeared. The steep hills that created the barrier grew smaller and smaller until they were nonexistent, and by nightfall, they were out of the pass and back into their own people's land.

The trio altered course to head toward their village, finding a suitable campsite to rest the night. They made a small fire and ate a freshly caught meal before turning in for the night, Leo taking the first watch.

Though they were out of the pass and in their own lands, Leo decided to rotate watch for the night, in case the Kiernane were still tracking them, but they had no surprises, and the night saw no battles.

The next morning they made their way toward their village, again without incident until near dusk when they ran into another band of Kiernane warriors. The hunting pack of six were hidden under heavy, thick brush, and the trio walked right past them at first, never even seeing them until one of the warriors leapt from their cover, tackling Slarn. The rest similarly revealed themselves with a pair howling war cries before joining their counterparts in the battle.

By the time the last two Kiernane warriors finished their howls, all three Feleine were scrambling to their feet or already fully engaged in combat. However, this time, after Fiera and Leo recovered, they didn't hesitate to go on the offensive. They downed the first of their opponents in seconds, attacking carelessly and leaving themselves open as they attacked. Their next opponents were dead just seconds later—the Kiernane, easy foes on a one-on-one fight.

Slarn was not so lucky. He managed to kill the warrior that tackled him, but his second opponent proved much more difficult because Slarn was at a significant disadvantage. Not only was he on the ground, but his first attacker had managed to take a well-placed bite out of his good arm just before the unprotected joint where his cuirass did not protect and somehow also managed to sink his axe through Slarn's armor into his side in the process.

The Kiernane that stood before him hesitated before striking Slarn, which saved Slarn's life, as the warrior brought its axe up slowly to relish in its kill but found an axe in its own back instead.

Leo rushed over to Slarn, retrieving his axe that he had thrown into his enemy's back, and knelt down.

"Slarn," he said.

"I will live," Slarn replied. "Thanks to you."

"Can you move?"

"Again, old friend, if it means I live, then I can move," Slarn replied as he used the elbow of his bandaged hand to sit up, wincing at the pain in his shoulder and bringing his good hand to his side.

Leo saw the blood oozing out of Slarn's side and lifted him up, pulling Slarn's handless arm around his neck, and guided Slarn to the closest tree, leaning him against it. Leo turned to Fiera.

"There are more of them coming. Start squishing the mushrooms over yourself. Hurry." Fiera quickly slid off her pack and did as ordered. "Fiera, we've got to split up. We will never outrun the Kiernane with Slarn in the shape that he is. I'll take him to Catron. It's closer than Cortin. Get back to Cortin and tell the council what's going on. If the Kiernane called for reinforcements, which is what they undoubtedly howled for, there will be a lot more Kiernane invading our lands. "I'll tell the council at Catron, if we make it there. Hopefully, Morlithis made it back before the Kiernane made it into our region. Now go."

Fiera didn't hesitate. She snatched up her pack, sliding it on as she finished spreading a mushroom over her, and raced off toward their village, Cortin.

Leo took Slarn over his shoulder and helped him through the forest in a hurry, not bothering to try and cover their scent. With Slarn bleeding as he was, no amount of mushroom would be able to cover their smell, so he just took Slarn over his shoulder, and the two made their way to Catron.

***

Fiera raced through trees, constantly scanning her surroundings as she hurried along, slowing to a walk to catch her breath every so often. Though she labored to breathe as she continued, she dared not stop to rest. She knew that she had to keep ahead of any Kiernane who might be able to track her. She feared that if she stopped, a hunting party might find her, so she kept walking until she could breathe more freely, and then she sped up to a run again until she couldn't breathe and started the whole cycle over again: walk, then run, then walk, then run, never stopping until she reached her village—thankfully with no further encounters.

***

Leo and Slarn, however, weren't so lucky. They traveled at a snail's pace, with Leo pulling Slarn along with one arm around Slarn's waist and the other holding Slarn's bandaged wrist around his neck. Slarn stumbled and hobbled his way through the forest, barely able to keep up with Leo's pace, though slow going it was for Leo. Slarn's fresh and bleeding wounds made for easy tracking, but Leo had neither the time nor more bandages to dress any of Slarn's injuries. Leo knew it was only a matter of time before the Kiernane caught up to them, and he only hoped they could make it to the village before then.

When the Kiernane finally did catch up to them, Slarn was unable even to lift a clawed hand. Leo refused to leave his friend—his brother—again. He would die rather than leave Slarn again, like he did the last time.

Leo dropped Slarn to the ground, ignoring the thump and moan from his friend, and unsheathed his axes. He dispatched one Kiernane and wounded another before one of the pack's axe blades penetrated Leo's armor and sent him to the ground with a gushing wound from his side.

Leo rolled to his back as the four uninjured warriors surrounded him, all raising their axes with deep grins on their faces.

Chapter ten

Morlithis woke, and when he opened his eyes, the blinding sunlight glared into his face, and he squinted. It took him a few seconds to adjust to the brightness of midday, but he could feel the softness of the bed he was lying in. He felt a cool breeze across his furry face, rustling his thick white whiskers, and he felt the soft fur blanket over him, covering him from the neck down.

His eyes finally adjusted to the light, and when he lifted his head to glance around the room, everything spun, and a shooting pain exploded in his skull. He dropped his head back onto the pillow and brought both hands to his head, moaning in agony.

He heard the creaking of a wooden floorboard, and he felt more than saw the Lithar, then it asked him if he spoke the common language with an almost hissing voice that prolonged the *s* sounds.

"I do," Morlithis replied, turning through a throbbing headache and dizziness to see its owner. It was a large gray-skinned Lithar, and though he couldn't tell the creature's gender from its appearance, he assumed it male as it had a deep raspy voice.

"You are in pain of the head," the Lithar said, noticing Morlithis's grimace and that he was clutching his head. "I will give you sssomething to lesssen the pain," he said as he walked over to Morlithis, snatching a bowl made of hollowed-out wood. He held the bowl up toward Morlithis. "If you drink thisss, the pain will leave," he said. "I will help." The creature lifted Morlithis's head up and slowly poured the liquid into Morlithis's mouth. Almost instantly, his headache diminished to a faint irritating throbbing.

Morlithis looked up at the large lizard-like man before him.

"It worked. I can tell in your face."

"It did," Morlithis replied. "Thank you."

"You are welcome. Now you ressst," the Lithar said and left.

Morlithis followed the creature with his eyes, noticing for the first time the Lithar's monk-like brown robes flowing in the breeze as the creature's tail wobbled side to side with its steps.

Morlithis saw as well that the entrance to his room was just an open archway with no door, and he could see outside. It looked bright and sunny. Too bright and sunny for him to be under the thick canopy of trees in the Lithar Canyon. These large gray Lithar must have taken him from the canyon. But the canyon was miles wide. Surely these creatures didn't carry him for miles.

He looked around the room, noticing the barren walls made from slats of wood nailed together with crude nails much like those his own people used. The walls had no decorations, but the array of planks made from different trees somewhat served as decoration, bringing a bit of color to the otherwise bland room with their shades of blacks, dark and light browns, and reds. The beams that held up the roof consisted of the same except Morlithis could see the black tar that sealed the cracks between the slats and beams. He assumed the tar sealant was to keep the rain out because the side walls had no such seal between the cracks.

The bed's blankets were animal fur, and the only other piece of furniture besides the bed was a single cushioned bench that appeared to be made for the bulky size of the gray Lithar.

His clothes were neatly laid on the bench, and that was when he realized that he was naked beneath the fur blankets. Naked except for the bandages around his shoulder and his injured hand. He flung the furs off the bed, suddenly worried about the catnip. The Lithar had undressed him and taken his supplies. His clothes were set out neatly, but his pack was nowhere to be seen.

He rushed over to his clothes, snatching them up quickly, his heart racing, fearing the catnip in his pack taken by these creatures.

He saw his pack then, as he bent over to grab his clothes. It was leaning on the opposite side of the bench. He had not seen it because it was hidden from his view when he was on the bed.

He dropped his clothes and snatched his pack up, frantically searching its contents for the pouch containing the catnip, and he sighed in relief as he found it. Sitting on the bench, his fur rustled in a sudden strong breeze that swept through the room, and he remembered that he was naked.

He donned his clothes and cuirass, noticing that the pain in his shoulder from the Kiernane bite was little more than a faint throbbing. He moved his arm in wide circles, testing his range of motion. Despite the faint throbbing, his shoulder was almost fully healed. At least, that is how it felt.

"You ssshould ressst," said a familiar voice in the common language, stretching the *s* sounds and startling Morlithis. He spun around to see the same Lithar—at least he thought it was the same—walking toward him with a bowl in his clawlike hands. "You not in danger," the Lithar said, seeing

109

Morlithis's reaction. "Eat." The lizard-like creature raised the bowl toward Morlithis.

Morlithis hesitated a moment, unsure about eating food given to him by such a race known for their savagery. He took the bowl, glancing around the room as he debated to himself whether a savage race would keep such living spaces and treat their prisoners with such kindness.

"Aren't you supposed to live in caves?" Morlithis asked, sniffing the bowl of stew, then spooning a bite.

"That isss the othersss," the Lithar replied.

"You mean the green Lithar?"

"Yesss."

"Are you Lithar also?" Morlithis asked as he took another spoonful of the stew.

"Yesss."

"Why have I never heard of you?"

"We do not travel. We ssstay here."

"But the others do. They travel and terrorize others."

"Yesss. We do not. We ssstay in our landsss."

Morlithis sat on the bench and continued sipping on the stew. "Why did you come to my rescue?"

"Did not mean to. You were jussst there."

"Why were you there?"

"It isss our land. The others want to take our land."

"You are at war?"

"Yesss. They want our land. We do not give it."

"I understand. Well, thank you for saving me."

"You are welcome."

Morlithis put the stew down on the bench. "I must be on my way. Am I a prisoner?" The Lithar looked at him, seemingly irritated.

"No," he said at last. "But you mussst ressst. You are weak from fight and injuriesss."

Morlithis looked back at the Lithar for a moment. "I will rest for a little while, but I must be on my way soon."

The Lithar nodded. "I leave you now to ressst." The Lithar turned and left. Morlithis followed him out with his eyes

111

again, then picked up the stew and walked over to the entryway. When he looked out over the porch, he was astonished.

He was still in the Lithara Canyon, but he was not in the wilds. He was in a large village. The trees had all been cut down, undoubtedly to create the homes and buildings that he saw. That was why he could see the sunlight so well. There were no trees to shade or block the light.

To one side of the town was the canyon wall, and he could see a thick wooden palisade fence with lookout towers at every corner. There was even a tower built into the cliff wall.

The town looked to be two or three times the size of his village and was heavily fortified along the palisade. The wooden fence looked—to Morlithis—as if an army would be hard-pressed to break through.

Within the walls of the small city, Morlithis could see what he assumed to be homes, a temple of some kind, and several larger buildings that he imagined were either royalty, military, or public gathering places.

Morlithis could see a dozen Lithar meandering across the village and a dozen more loitering here and there. A lake stood at the end of the town, against the valley's cliffside, the palisade walls stretching around it, enclosing it inside their village.

An arena near the lake caught his eye, and he suddenly remembered the arrows that downed several of his opponents before he was knocked out. He would recognize an archery range anywhere.

It was only a few dozen yards, and he could easily see the rows of targets lined up and the Lithar practicing.

He decided that he would venture a closer peek at their archery range before he left.

As he neared, he could hear the thud of arrows sinking into wooden targets, the plopping of novice archers' bracers, and the swish of the arrows shooting through the air. It reminded him of the days back home when he practiced.

He smiled at the young Lithar learning to wield their bows as they stopped and stared at him, then their trainers prodded them back on task, giving Morlithis a glance of their own.

He felt calm on the range. It was the one place that relaxed him, and he knew that he should feel self-conscious because the Lithar kept eyeing him between shots, but he wasn't.

A loud, deep, reverberating horn sounded, and the Lithar village erupted with a flurry of motion. The Lithar trainers bounded away, leaving their trainees alone, and those loitering hurried to the nearest palisade stairs. Lithar from their homes raced onto the palisade, and a dozen rushed from the larger buildings to the palisade walls.

Another dozen sprinted as fast as their bulky frames allowed back and forth between what Morlithis assumed to be an armory and the palisade. They each carried handfuls of quivers from the armory and ran along a section of the palisade, dropping a quiver every few feet. When they were out, they returned to the armory for another handful of quivers.

Morlithis was impressed with the efficiency of the Lithar as they readied to defend their village. Morlithis watched for only a few moments before deciding to join the ranks of archers

to defend the walls.

Chapter eleven

Morlithis raced over to the armory, pausing momentarily to find the bows and arrows, and rushed over to the wooden rack that housed the quivers. He snatched up a quiver, sliding the shoulder strap over his head as he raced by on his way to the sparse collection of bows, and inspected each bow with a glance, finally choosing a thick reddish-black bow that appeared to be freshly polished.

He snatched the bow from the rack and hurried back down the aisle, grabbing another quiver on his way out. He ran along the base of the palisade wall until he reached the closest staircase and rushed up it, ignoring the looks from the younger Lithar as they ran past him to stock more quivers along the palisade walls.

The Lithar were already fully engaged in battle, stringing arrow after arrow and sending them flying. When Morlithis squeezed into formation, the most reaction he received was a look in his direction and a nod from his neighboring Lithar companions.

When Morlithis looked out onto the battlefield, he couldn't help but pause for just a moment at the majestic awe of what he saw before him.

An open field spanned the length of the village several hundred yards out. Beyond that, the Lithar forest, grown thick and lush.

The blue sky, heavy with cloud cover that floated by like islands float by a ship, contrasted with the greens of the land, adding to its beauty, and the shadows of the clouds rolled along the open plane as if they were shadows of invisible ships in the ocean.

Among the calming beauty of nature, however, was the chaos of battle. The smaller green Lithar swarmed the open plain by the hundreds, and by the hundreds fell. Dark streaks filled the sky as the arrows arched through the sky, sinking deep into the chests of the attacking Lithar or finding empty field to sink into, and the Lithar charged with a roar of hissing that sounded like rushing water.

By the time the green Lithar reached the walls, only a handful of their ranks were left, but they kept pouring out of the forest, sacrificing themselves in a hopeless attempt to take the gray Lithar's home.

Morlithis began firing, downing Lithar after Lithar with precision as they neared the walls. Then from out of the trees rolled a catapult manned by not the small green Lithar, but humans.

Humans were rare in these lands, except for the occasional adventurer band; they tended to stay close to the trading routes, but these were no adventurers. These humans were soldiers. A score of humans stepped out from the safety of the trees with half a dozen catapults.

As he fired several more arrows, Morlithis wondered what kind of humans would ally themselves with these wicked Lithar and what their purpose for such an alliance would be.

The enormous wooden catapult released, sending a heavy boulder flying. The rock hit the wooden barrier just a few yards away, tearing through the wooden fence with a loud thundering crack, and Morlithis felt the palisade wall waver where he stood.

A dozen Lithar tumbled to the ground amid the wood rubble.

"We have to take out those devices!" Morlithis said in the common tongue to the Lithar beside him. "Do you have anything that will reach that far?" Morlithis asked the Lithar to his right.

The Lithar shook his head no. Morlithis looked back over the battlefield, noticing it was only the humans that manned the catapults.

"Listen," he said, turning to back to the Lithar. "You have to tell whoever is in charge that we need to go out there and kill those humans. They are the ones operating those machines."

The Lithar nodded. "Come," he said, leaving his post. Morlithis followed the Lithar down the staircase that he had run up before, along the base of the fortification, across the rubble of the destroyed section of the fence, and back up another set of stairs.

By the time that Morlithis crossed the new hole made by the catapult, the green Lithar were already converging on the opening, and though they found their deaths at the sharp ends of arrows, Morlithis knew it was only a matter of time before the green Lithar made it past the walls.

The Lithar Morlithis was following stopped behind another robed Lithar and spoke something in Lithar. The robed Lithar turned to Morlithis.

Though the Lithar all looked almost identical to Morlithis, they had slight differences in appearance. A larger or shorter snout, lighter or darker hide, different eye color or voice, or a myriad of subtle details that set them apart from their counterparts. Morlithis was positive that this robed Lithar was the very same that had met with him upon his waking.

"Thisss isss not your war. Why help usss?" he said.

"Because I'm here to be able to help. Besides, you helped me. We can consider this me returning your kindness."

"What isss it you propossse?"

"We need to get archers close enough to kill the humans that are using those machines. I don't think the Lithar know how to use them. If we can take out all of the humans, then they won't be able to use the machines anymore."

"The humansss are too far."

"I know. That's why we must go outside the gates. We need to get close enough to kill them."

"But that will take Lithar from wall."

"I know, but look." Morlithis pointed to the catapults. "They are reloading the machines, and they will be firing again any moment now. You can't afford not to at least try and take them out."

The Lithar looked at the catapults and back at Morlithis and nodded.

"I will do."

"Good. I'm going with you to help, but first I need to get my pack. I have to try and make it back to my own people."

"We will wait."

"No. I will catch up. You must act fast, or your village will be lost."

"We will go now!" the Lithar replied and turned to the Lithar that escorted Morlithis, speaking Lithar to him.

Morlithis spun around and raced back across the palisade wall, down the steps, and across the village to the hut he awoke in. Checking to make sure the catnip was still tucked safely in his pack, he slid it on. Once he had his pack secured, he darted back out of the hut and back across the village courtyard, calling over a young Lithar carrying a full quiver. Morlithis snatched the arrows out of the Lithar's quiver and shoved them into his near-empty one, then raced off toward the hole in the palisade fence and onto the battlefield.

Chapter twelve

Morlithis jumped over green Lithar corpse after green Lithar corpse as he ran headlong into the throes of battle. He fired shot after shot after shot with his bow as he raced across the green grassland. His quiver quickly emptied, and as he reached back for another arrow, he discovered that he had spent his last precious projectile without realizing it. His foe had spotted him and already began charging toward him, hissing a defiant call to his counterparts. Morlithis's eyes darted to the three green Lithar who now joined his enemy.

For the first time since he rushed into this battle, he noticed the overwhelming forces of the enemy surrounding him.

The three green Lithar were closing in with remarkable speed, lifting their spiked clubs, preparing for their blows. Morlithis heard the unmistakable swish of arrows whizzing by, and the next instant, he saw the arrows protruding from the chests of the three Lithar only feet from him.

Morlithis hadn't traveled that far from the palisade and had not yet caught up with the gray Lithar, so he turned a quick glance back toward the palisade and a thank-you salute to the Lithar manning the wall, then rushed to yank an arrow from the chest of the nearest fresh corpse, nocking and loosing the arrow in one swift motion.

The field was now in plenty of both corpses and arrows as more and more green Lithar fell dead with arrows protruding from their chests, and with no time to waste, Morlithis didn't take the extra effort to replenish his quiver. Instead, he yanked arrows from the fallen green Lithar, nocking and loosing them swiftly into nearby enemies as he made his way toward his counterparts.

On several occasions, before he reached his counterparts, swiftly cutting through the green Lithar ranks, the gray Lithar archers from the palisade wall saved his life as a small horde of enemy Lithar advanced on him.

When he finally reached his fellow Lithar, they were out of range of their allies on the wall and the horde pressed in. He

126

quickly inserted himself into the last position of the archery line, noticing as he neared that several dozen gray Lithar marched just a few paces ahead of the archers' line with spears.

Morlithis understood now how his allies could traverse the battleground so fast amid the overwhelming enemy army. The formation was immaculate, with spear wielders at the front, archers giving cover for them, and a second row of archers covering the rear flanks of the line. A truly skilled, practiced, and precise formation, indeed. Morlithis wondered how the rear row of archers didn't trip or bump the archers in front of them, as they never missed a step, all while marching backward.

The green Lithar poured in from the tree line, several hundred attacking, thinking Morlithis and his small band of Lithar warriors easy prey so far from reinforcements. They didn't live long enough to learn from their mistake. Morlithis's allies, skilled as they were, felled their adversaries quickly, continuing their march until they were out of arrows as well.

The gray Lithar, being less agile than the green Lithar, did not attempt swift attacks with their spears but instead executed calculated and slow deceptive attacks. One Lithar jabbed at his smaller foe, not with the intention of harm, but as a distraction, as another sank its javelin point into the side of their foe. Half of the time, the deceptively fast green Lithar impaled itself onto its enemy's spear as it dodged an attack from another gray Lithar.

Morlithis marveled at the skill of these clumsy and slow creatures as they fought with such cunning, ferocity, and efficiency, and that, as of yet, none had fallen, despite the overwhelming number of enemies.

As the archers fired their last arrows, they slid their bows over their heads, resting their weapons across their chests, and pulled out a pair of short spears from pouches along the sides of their quivers. Only a dozen gray Lithar continued to fire arrows, bounding from green Lithar corpse to Green Lithar corpse, yanking, nocking, and loosing arrow after arrow as the line formation broke off into small groups that formed protective circles around the archers. Again, Morlithis marveled at the harmony in which they fought together, anticipating their allies' thrusts and attacks as they worked in unison, keeping at bay the horde of enemy Lithar.

Morlithis, skilled in his own ranged combat style and much more agile than his allies, needed little protection when recycling arrows. Unlike his Lithar counterparts, he yanked, nocked, and loosed the arrows in a single swift motion in a third of the time the Lithar archers did. While the Lithars' bulky frames didn't allow for them to roll, dive, or run swiftly, Morlithis's agility gave him speed and maneuverability greater than that of even the green Lithar.

As the spear wielders managed to dispatch most of the attacking Lithar, Morlithis circled his companions, loosing arrow after arrow into nearby Lithar. When a green Lithar made it through his allies' protective circles, the archers dispatched them quickly with precision between loosing arrows into enemies beyond the Lithar circles.

The chaos of battle was extensive beyond the range of the Lithar archers at the palisade. The green Lithar continued to rush through the tree line like a flood as they neared closer and closer to the catapults, swarming the small band as they continued to attack, and Morlithis knew that they would soon be overrun, despite the impressive skill of his counterparts.

Then he saw a score of green Lithar fall to their deaths with arrows in their chests. Morlithis dared a quick glance back toward the Lithar village to see a second wave of Lithar spearmen and archers nearing. He dared a further glance up to the top of the palisade, noticing half of the archers missing.

Morlithis didn't question the strategy, as he knew the Lithar tactics were superior, and so he returned to battle, just in time to send an arrow into the chest of a dangerously close green Lithar.

The ally reinforcements gave Morlithis's party the advantage they needed. Soon the men manning the catapults were dead, and the small band of Lithar warriors raced for the next catapult. After the first two were destroyed, the green Lithar began retreating, their numbers already decimated, and without the green Lithar to protect the humans and their catapults, the surviving humans fled into the forest as well, abandoning their siege weapons.

As the last of the horde fled, Morlithis finally took the time to take a better look at the now corpse-filled open grassland and saw among the thousands of corpses a dozen clusters of archers and spearmen huddled in formations throughout the grassland, hissing cheers as their foes retreated.

"You fight well." Morlithis turned to see the Lithar that fought beside him on the wall. At least, as far as he could tell it was him.

"Thank you." Morlithis nodded. "I have never seen such skill as your people have in battle."

The Lithar nodded a thank-you as well. "Lithar not ssso ssskilled asss green Lithar bad fightersss," the Lithar said, curling up the corners of his snout in what Morlithis could only assume was a smile.

"Nevertheless, your skills are impressive," Morlithis replied with a smile of his own.

"You sssay you mussst leave?" the Lithar asked.

"Yes, I must find my way back to my village."

"We will guide you sssome waysss." The Lithar waved over a fellow Lithar with an unusually dark hide compared to the rest of the Lithar that he had seen, and spoke to him in his native tongue. The Lithar nodded and bounded off. "To help keep you sssafe. Wait a moment," the Lithar finished.

A few moments later, the dark-hided Lithar who left returned with three full quivers, handing one to Morlithis and another to the Lithar who spoke to Morlithis, then swapped his own empty quiver out for the full one.

"You keep bow, and we go now, yesss?" the Lithar asked as he switched quivers, handing the empty one to his counterpart.

"Thank you." Morlithis nodded. "Yes, we go now," he replied and followed suit, handing the empty quiver to the Lithar, who gave it to the dark-hided Lithar, who in turn tossed the three empty quivers to a fellow counterpart nearby.

"Come," the Lithar replied and headed into the forest.

Morlithis didn't hesitate to follow.

Chapter thirteen

Morlithis followed without question the two Lithar guiding him. They led him around the edge of the clearing of their land, not venturing far from the tree line that marked their territory until they reached the towering canyon wall.

"We mussst ressst here before continuing," the Lithar who had fought beside him said as he slid his quiver off and set his bow against the wall. "And eat for the journey ahead." He nodded to the dark-hided Lithar, who disappeared deeper into the forest, returning with three large orange-and-yellow-striped fruits moments later.

"Eat," he said as he tossed one to Morlithis and another to his counterpart. Morlithis noticed the scratchiness in his voice, then saw the scar at his neck several shades lighter than the rest of him.

"Thank you," Morlithis said, still standing, and sniffed the large grapefruit, then made his way over to sit next to the two Lithar, setting his bow and quiver next to him. "So, uh, what are

135

your names?" Morlithis asked as he clawed out a portion of the fruit.

"In your tongue, my name would translate to Dratheer," replied the lighter-hided of his companions.

"Agarathar," said the dark-hided Lithar. "It meansss dark one."

"Morlithis," Morlithis replied and stuffed the piece of fruit into his mouth. "Thank you for guiding me," he said with a mouthful.

"You are welcome. Thisss canyon hasss many dangersss, and green Lithar. Sssafessst not to travel alone," replied Dratheer.

"I see. I welcome the help and company."

Dratheer nodded, and the three continued eating their fruit.

Morlithis studied the two Lithar as he ate, noticing that Agarathar's snout was much thinner than Dratheer's and his eyes matched his dark gray hide. Both had similar builds, but Agarathar's tail was narrower, and his clawed hands appeared more deadly. Morlithis couldn't help but stare at the scar on Agarathar's neck, wondering what had happened to this warrior to give him such a scar.

"He won the battle," Dratheer commented.

"What?" Morlithis replied, turning his attention to Dratheer.

"You are ssstaring at Agarathar'sss ssscar. He won the battle with the beassst that gave him the ssscar."

"It must have hurt," Morlithis replied, turning his gaze to Agarathar. "Sorry for staring."

"No offenssse is taken," Dratheer replied. "Agarathar ssspeaks little now. Ssscar is painful when ssspeaking."

"What creature was it that gave you the scar?" Morlithis asked.

"A dangerousss rodent that inhabitsss the treesss," Dratheer replied. "One of many dangersss in the canyon."

"I see. I will keep an eye on the treetops," Morlithis replied.

"Creature only awake at night. No danger asss long asss you ssstay near wall," Dratheer informed.

"What other dangers must I be wary of?" Morlithis asked.

"Ssstay near wall and dangersss ssstay away," Dratheer answered.

"Understood. I will stay near the wall, then," Morlithis commented. "That is why you brought me here to eat."

"Yesss," Dratheer replied after finishing his bite. "Sssafessst by wall. We only need to look that way for danger." Dratheer waved his arm around the open forest. "Only three directionssss." Dratheer stood. "Let usss go now."

***

The three traveled along the canyon wall quietly. They had traveled much of the day, and Dratheer had explained that enemy Lithar would be scouting the forest here, so they needed to be as silent as possible. They kept an eye on the forest as they walked and listened for any sounds that might indicate danger.

Forest animals scurried away as they neared, and birds fluttered into the sky, but they had not—as of yet—met any hostility.

They came upon a pond that opened from the mouth of a cave in the canyon wall, and they stopped.

"Fill," Dratheer said, lifting a waterskin. Morlithis wondered where the skin had come from, as he did not recall Dratheer having one earlier, but set aside the thought, realizing just how thirsty he was upon seeing the pond.

Morlithis slid his quiver off his back, realizing only then how awkward he must have appeared to the two Lithar who carried only their quivers and bows. Morlithis, on the other hand, wore his leather armor, his bow, his quiver, and his pack. Though his pack, as full as it was, rested snugly against his quiver, it did not inhibit his ability to snatch arrows if he needed them. The pack was bulky and heavy, though he was used to the added weight, and he barely noticed it.

Morlithis slid his pack off next and rummaged through it until he found his waterskin. It still had some water in it, but he uncorked it and poured its contents onto the forest floor anyway, then knelt at the edge of the pond and held the waterskin under the water until it stopped bubbling.

"Morlithisss," he heard Dratheer say and turned to see Dratheer holding his waterskin out in one hand and his quiver out in the other. Dratheer set the waterskin into a pouch that sat in the center of the quiver. Morlithis's eyes went wide at seeing the ingenuity that the Lithar had with their quivers. "Water pouch inssside," Dratheer said as he showed Morlithis a small string he pulled tight and tied.

Morlithis snatched up his quiver and examined it, noticing that it did indeed have a pouch that held a waterskin. He had never even noticed that the quivers contained pouches. As he marveled at the design, he could understand how anyone could have missed the pouch. The quivers were expertly made. This quiver was made of leather dyed a deep brown with stitching around the pouch to match. Again, the hidden side panels that held the short spears were marked only by the stitching, and a small latch on the bottom enabled the bases to slide out, releasing the short spears.

140

"Your people have exquisite skill and ingenuity," Morlithis said.

"Thisss," Dratheer held up the quiver, "isss much easssier to carry than your packsss."

"Indeed, it is," Morlithis replied as he filled the waterskin. "Next, you're going to tell me that you have food rations hidden in there."

"Yesss. Thisss isss posssible, but not in thessse onesss," Dratheer replied.

Morlithis looked up. "Well, that doesn't surprise me," he said as he stood.

He was about to say something more when the three heard a rustling in the trees. Morlithis shifted his weight, turning toward the sound, which saved his life as an arrow swooshed past him, bouncing off the canyon wall. Morlithis's training kicked in, and he dove for his quiver and bow, dropping the waterskin, and rolled to his feet, snatching up his bow and quiver as he stood.

The two Lithar bounded over to large trees, taking cover behind them.

Morlithis darted behind a tree as well, dropping his quiver and nocking an arrow.

The three peered into the surrounding forest, scanning for the bowman, but he was too well hidden.

"Thisss not green Lithar," Agarathar said. "Lithar do not ussse bowsss."

"Try and draw this fire but be careful. I have an idea," Morlithis ordered, snatching up his quiver again, keeping his arrow nocked, and crouching his way deeper into the forest.

Agarathar and Dratheer peeked their heads out from behind their trees only to be met by an arrow flying toward each of them.

"I sssee him," Agarathar replied.

"I sssee one alssso. At leassst two, I sssee," Dratheer said.

***

Morlithis hurried through the trees in a low crouch as fast as he could, then circled his way out away from the canyon wall, scanning the forest floor and the trees above fiercely for even the slightest signs of movement.

He found shortly a single bowman facing the pond, and he froze, crouching even lower. He scanned the forest slowly for more archers, seeing two more. Morlithis inched slowly to the side to get a clearer aim on the first of his targets. He saw the enemy preparing for another shot toward the pond and brought his bow up quickly, letting his arrow fly before the bowman could loose his arrow. Morlithis's arrow hit its mark.

The two remaining bowmen each let out an arrow toward Morlithis's counterparts, then, seeing their fellow fall, both turned their attention to Morlithis.

***

Agarathar and Dratheer peeked their heads out a second time, receiving another arrow fired at each of them. Both ducked behind their respective trees again. That was all they needed, an instant to pinpoint their attackers' locations. The first enemy volley sent toward them told them where to look, and the second told them where to aim. They both now knew precisely where to aim. Both prepared their bows, nocking an arrow. Both stepped out fully from their cover. Both loosed their arrows. Both felt the piercing sting of an enemy arrow sinking deep into their hides.

***

Morlithis saw the two archers notice him and saw the arrows that sank into both. Morlithis didn't have time to rejoice at the victory, however, as he noticed movement just a few yards deeper into the forest, and when he focused his attention on that movement, fear and panic gripped him yet again, and all the memories of his cowardice resurfaced.

Chapter fourteen

Morlithis raced back to Agarathar and Dratheer. His heart was beating so fast and hard in his chest it seemed like that was all that he could hear. He didn't dare glance back at the dozens of Lithar and human archers chasing him. All he wanted to do was flee, but he had to warn his Lithar companions first.

"Agarathar, Dratheer, we have to go!" he screamed as he neared the pond where they had been ambushed. Then, as he emerged from the brush, he saw his two counterparts lying on the canyon floor with an arrow protruding from each of them.

Morlithis didn't notice that the arrows were not fatal. All he saw were two arrows in his companions, plus the impending doom of over thirty enemy troops moments away from slaughtering him. He could think only to run, and so he did. He darted around the edge of the small pond, jumping over Agarathar as he fled.

Agarathar moaned, lifting an arm as Morlithis passed. At first, Morlithis was so panicked that he almost missed seeing

Agarathar move, but just as he finished skirting the pond, his senses caught up to him, and he paused.

He looked back toward the two gray-skinned Lithar, seeing both now moving. Morlithis was about to abandon his counterparts and, in fact, took a couple of steps before stopping. His thoughts jumped back to his first encounter with the Kiernane. When he rushed away from his party and was caught alone, he remembered how Leo, Fiera, and Slarn didn't hesitate to jump headlong into battle, Slarn losing a hand in the process.

Morlithis spun back around, racing over to Agarathar, helping him up, then rushed over to Dratheer, who had already pulled himself most of the way up.

"We have to leave! There are thirty or more men advancing on us. There is no way that we can defend ourselves against that many! They'll be here any second."

"Can you swim?" Dratheer asked.

"What does that—? Uh, yes, but—"

"Follow us," Dratheer interrupted as he snapped off the end of the arrow from his thigh and dove into the pond.

146

Agarathar followed suit, snapping off the end of the arrow lodged in his shoulder and diving into the pond.

Morlithis hesitated a moment, took a big breath, then dove in after them.

The water was clear, and Morlithis had no trouble seeing the two Lithar racing away from him. Morlithis followed the two into a tunnel that led through the canyon wall, and as he swam farther into the underwater cavern, darkness quickly came, allowing his dark vision to take over. He could feel the cave ceiling just inches above his head, and he saw where the tunnel opened back up. He followed his companions as fast as he could swim, but he could not keep up with his lizard-like counterparts. Morlithis knew he couldn't hold his breath for much longer and swam with all his strength to reach the opening before he drowned. He could feel the almost pain-like sensations as he began to suffocate. His lungs heaved faster and faster in desperate attempts for air, and he pushed down the instinct to open his mouth as his lungs quaked in shorter and shorter increments, then he reached the opening, and with a renewed vigor and clarity, he kicked and pushed as fast and hard as he could up into the opening, gasping for air as his furry head burst out of the water.

"Ressst over there," Dratheer said, seeing Morlithis emerge from the water, and pointed to a ledge several feet away. "We will remove arrowsss and bandage oursssselvesss alssso."

Morlithis nodded and swam to the ledge, pulling himself onto the platform while Dratheer and Agarathar climbed quickly out of the water, using their tails for an extra push, lifting them out of the water as they swam.

Morlithis sat on the ledge for several minutes while his companions tended to their injuries. He noticed the faint light seeping in from an opening at the far side of the cavern, which allowed him to see with the dull grays of his dark vision. The opening was beyond a steep slope that ended with a sheer jagged wall. The cavern itself was several yards long, and there was another tunnel just a few feet away with a sliver of light shining through as well.

Morlithis heard a splash and jumped to his feet, readying his bow.

"We are sssafe from enemiesss here," Dratheer said. "Lithar too afraid and humansss not want to drown."

"I understand. I almost drowned."

"Only bad ssswimmersss drown," Agarathar replied, the corners of his snout slightly rising, revealing his teeth. The equivalent of a Lithar smile, Morlithis presumed.

Morlithis shook off the excess water from his fur, splattering the two Lithar, and the two brought a hand to shield their faces. "Well, my people despise getting wet, so I guess we are all bad swimmers.

Morlithis changed the subject. "So, do we just wait here and then swim back, hoping they are gone?"

"No. We take that way." Dratheer pointed to the tunnel near them. "It will take usss sssafely to another opening in canyon wall. We will leave you then."

***

149

The three hiked single file through the small cave tunnel, Dratheer leading and Agarathar in the rear. Morlithis said almost nothing the entire time, now having plenty of time to consider his actions at the pond. Again, Morlithis's cowardice revealed itself. This time not only was it his cowardice that he dealt with, but due to his cowardice, he almost sacrificed the lives of Dratheer and Agarathar. He almost left them to die, knowing that they were still alive. It didn't matter that they might have escaped through the underwater passage. He didn't know about the passage then. He just wanted to save himself.

They reached the cavern exit, and Dratheer stopped. Morlithis had been so engrossed in his thoughts that he never noticed the transition from the dull grays of his dark vision to the vibrant colors of his normal vision.

"We are here. We mussst leave you now." Morlithis nodded, and Dratheer stepped to the side, allowing Morlithis to squeeze by.

"You have been sssilent," Dratheer said.

"Have I?"

"You have been pondering your actionsss at the pond," Agarathar said. Morlithis looked at Agarathar.

"I did not realize that you knew what I did, yes."

"Why?" Dratheer asked.

"I was going to leave you. I was too afraid. I was going to let you die."

"But you did not," Agarathar replied.

"But I was going to."

"What mattersss isss that you did not," Agarathar replied.

"We all have fear," Dratheer said. "When we fight our fear, we become better warriorsss. When we allow fear to take usss, then we act againssst our better nature as warriors. Cowardice isss sssimply not controlling our fear. If we do not control our fear, it will control usss. In the end, you took control of your fear and decided to ssstay, knowing that you may die—that isss bravery. Fear helpsss usss, but if not controlled, it can destroy usss too. Let it guide you but not control you."

151

Morlithis nodded. "I will not let fear control me. You both are wise warriors, and I am honored to call you friends."

"Asss are we," Dratheer said. "Few Lithar travel thisss far. Ssstay near wall until river nearsss wall. Do not cross river. Many dangersss acrosss river. You will be sssafe until canyon wall endsss."

"Thank you. I will not cross the river."

"Go now. Dark comes soon." Morlithis nodded and climbed down the canyon cliff. The tunnel entrance was only a few dozen feet from the ground, so it didn't take Morlithis long to climb down.

"Morlithis," Dratheer called. "Do not forget again," he said and tossed a waterskin to Morlithis.

"Thank you," Morlithis replied with a grin. "You have proven too generous yet again with the water. I will repay you someday if I can."

Dratheer and Agarathar lifted an arm in farewell and disappeared back into the cave entrance.

Morlithis slung the waterskin around his shoulder, repositioning his bow so that the waterskin would not hinder him from removing his bow if he needed to use it.

Chapter fifteen

Morlithis kept near the canyon wall as he finished the day's travel. He had been pondering what his Lithar companions discussed with him.

He still felt ashamed of what he had done. He still felt cowardly despite his decision to stay and fight with them. Morlithis wondered how he could ever trust himself not to abandon his allies. He wondered if the temptation to desert his counterparts would arise again. He pondered, if it came down to choosing to stand by his fellow warriors or abandoning those he claimed to care for in their direst need, which would he choose?

It was dusk and getting darker by the minute, and the warning of the nocturnal beasts that roamed the night rang in his ears, so he kept his senses alert. Alert for both these creatures of the night and a cleft or ridge to rest, though he doubted he would sleep easily this night. He knew from experience that the canyon was dangerous during the daytime. How much more threatening was it at night?

After a while, he quit looking for a good rest site and focused on the forest. He heard the skittering of small animals and the sounds of larger creatures rustling the bushes and trees, but none of the forest noises stirred him. Not like when the wolves were stalking him.

He heard a howl and froze in mid-stride, straining his ears for any indication that he was in danger. After a moment, a second howl and then a third cut through the night, but none sounded close. Still, Morlithis picked up his pace, not wanting to spend a second longer than he needed to in the canyon. He decided to go without sleep until he reached his people's lands.

***

Morning came, and Morlithis could feel the exhaustion setting in. He hadn't stopped to rest all night, nor had he eaten. His waterskin was nearly empty, but he dared not venture away from the wall during the night, and now that daybreak had come, he moved deeper into the forest toward the river, which he was not to cross. He constantly felt unease. Maybe it was his past few days' experience in this canyon, or perhaps it was that he knew so little of the dangers in this place, or that he was alone and knew there could be enemies hunting him, but he always felt like he was in peril. It was an unsettling feeling to always feel vulnerable, and he wanted nothing more than to end that feeling. Getting back to his own people's lands would end this constant feeling of danger and vulnerability, he knew, and so when he found another striped fruit, he ate it while he walked, wanting as little time as possible in the canyon.

When he finally did reach the river, daylight had fully come, and though he could still hear the scurrying critters and the rustling bushes nearby, they did not concern him much.

The river itself flowed swiftly with clear water that churned amid the protruding rocks, with white bubbles that disappeared as quickly as they appeared.

He saw no fish in the water as he bent low to fill his waterskin, but he felt the cool breeze brought on from the slight mist created from the churning water. Though he had been traveling and fighting in the canyon for days now, he hadn't realized how warm it was until now, even in the shade of the trees. The cooling mist was welcome, and he sat at the bank of the small river enjoying the coolness it brought.

His eyes went wide, and his mouth dropped when he glanced up at the other side of the river and saw a field of catnip blanketing the riverbank for as far as he could see in either direction. The catnip rose even up a small hill and into the forest. Morlithis stood to his feet, his heart pounding in his chest with excitement. If he just grabbed the catnip on the bank of the river, he could bring enough back to treat more than just the priest king. Just a few handfuls would be enough to treat his whole village.

Dratheer and Agarathar had warned him about crossing the river, but surely there was little danger at the bank, he thought. He could just stay near the bank. When he scanned the forest for any signs of a threat, he could only see the greens and browns of the forest trees. No animals and no signs of danger at all, so he decided to venture quickly to the other side of the bank for a few moments to grab just a few handfuls of the catnip and return across the river.

He peered into the depths of the river, noticing that it was only a few feet deep at the bank, and the river itself did not look very menacing with its small rapids. He knew that he could cross it easily, and he jumped in, feeling the cold water rush over the edge of his boots, quickly soaking through his leggings up to the knees. As he stepped farther and farther into the river, the cold rushing water soaking into his clothes caused Morlithis to shiver from the sudden temperature change. When the water reached his chest, he found himself breathing short, fast breaths as it shocked his system. The higher the water rose on his body, the more he had to adjust his weight as he made his way across to keep from being knocked over by the current.

As quickly as his body was shocked by the temperature change, it became used to the cold. By the time Morlithis climbed up the other side, he was no longer shivering, but the forest breeze sent slight chills down his spine as gusts of wind that had previously gone unnoticed suddenly felt frigid as it collided with his cold, wet fur. He shook off the excess water from his coat, showering the nearby catnip and trees with

159

projectiles of droplets. When he finished, he began pulling up the catnip, keeping sure to stay near the bank of the river.

He heard movement in the trees above and spun, staring up at the trees overhead. Seeing nothing, he turned back to pulling catnip and shoving it into his pack.

He soon found himself just a few feet away from the riverbank and heard a noise again from the treetops. He decided to return to the other side of the river, remembering the warnings.

When he turned back toward the bank, a thin glistening string of webs wafted in front of his face, and he brushed them away, then wiped his hand on his breeches as the web tickled his hands furiously before they flew away in another gust of wind.

Morlithis barely took two more steps before noticing his hand going numb and stopped. When he brought his hand up to his face to investigate, he saw a clump of the shimmering webbing drifting toward him again and waved it away. This time the webbing wasn't as easy to wave off. Morlithis's waving served only to spread the individual strands out, and several brushed over his forearm while more fell onto his cuirass before drifting off into the wind.

Morlithis brushed off the strands on his cuirass, noticing that now his forearm was going numb.

"What is this?" Morlithis asked to himself, beginning to panic. "What's going on?"

As if in answer, a flurry of movement erupted from the trees overhead.

Morlithis heard the creatures before he saw them.

They climbed from limb to limb of the trees toward him, then jumped down onto the forest floor and charged. Their round, green, leaflike fur abdomens and hard, bark-like, brown, triangular heads bobbed up and down as their six boney legs scampered across the forest floor, and their three barbed tails jabbed at the air in anticipation. Horns littered their heads, and their eyes filled the whole of the sides of their triangular heads, protected by even more horns that curved toward the beasts' eyes. Two were a foot in diameter, and the third was almost triple that height, with its abdomen standing at least knee-high.

161

Its triangular head added even more height to its menacing appearance.

Their leaflike fur and bark-like triangular heads allowed them to blend with the trees, but on the ground with less cover and camouflage, Morlithis could see these creatures plain as day, and with the sight of these nightmarish beasts came a dread and terror the likes of which he had never felt before.

Chapter sixteen

Morlithis stumbled backward as the spiderlike creatures advanced. He yanked his bow from around his neck and desperately reached for his arrows with his numb hand. The beasts were closing fast, and he knew that he had little time, but he had no feeling in his hand nor his forearm. He couldn't tell if he was gripping an arrow or not.

The three creatures flanked him, the two smaller spider creatures swinging around to attack him from the sides as the larger one slowed, spitting its webbing at him. The web was more concentrated this time and shot through the air like a net, flying straight for his face.

Morlithis only saw the glistening silklike string through the corner of his eye as he twisted his neck sideways and strained his eyes to see the arrows behind his back out of the opposite corner of his eye because of the webbing shimmering in the light.

It had only taken seconds, but in those few seconds he was able to turn his head, strain his eyes, and finally see that he did have a hold on one of his arrows. Morlithis turned just in time to bring his bow up and catch the silklike strings as they wrapped around the top edge of his bow. A second later, the first of the spidery creatures flanking him lunged at him.

Morlithis, seeing the beast leap into the air, twisted his body, bringing his numb forearm up, knocking it to the side, and both tumbled to the forest floor.

The moment Morlithis fell to the ground, he rolled to his knees, scanning the forest floor for his foes. He saw only the large one and the second smaller one but heard a splash accompanied by a squeal and more splashing.

He didn't have time to investigate further his assumption that the spiderlike beast fell into the stream as the two creatures left scrambled toward him. Morlithis, still not able to feel his forearm or hand, glanced down to make sure that he was still holding his arrow and did the only thing that he could think of to save his life—if it saved his life.

Slarn woke to the warm, gentle hug of a rabbit fur blanket. He was in a soft bed in a dark room with only one window that stood open at the far wall from his bed that let in the light. His hand—or rather, his nub—itched, burned, and stung all at the same time, and when he looked down at his bare arm, he saw why. His wrist was bandaged with fresh gauze and ointment, and he could feel the stiffness that accompanied cauterization.

"Ah, my friend. You have finally woken," he heard Leo say. And when Slarn turned to his friend, he saw that Leo too was bandaged.

Leo had a bandage across his chest with a thick pad of gauze at his side.

"Where are we?" Slarn asked as Leo walked over from the chair he was sitting in.

"We are in Catron."

"How did we get here? Last I remember, you were dropping me, and the Kiernane were chasing us.

Leo smiled.

165

"Yes. Sorry about that. The Kiernane caught up with us and, well." Leo motioned to his bandages. "They attacked. We made it close enough to Catron that a patrol found and rescued us before the Kiernane cut us down."

"Patrol? Why?"

"Well, it seems, lucky for us, that a lot more Kiernane have invaded our lands than we thought, and they aren't too stealthy of a race, you know. So, several packs were discovered in our lands, and Catron started sending patrols.

"I see. Lucky indeed."

"Yes."

"How long have I been asleep?"

Two days, my friend. You were not doing so good."

"Two days!" Slarn said as he sat up. "We must leave at once. We must warn Cortin."

"Relax, my friend," Leo said, resting a hand on Slarn's shoulder. "Word has already been sent to all of the villages of the Kiernane invasion. You need to rest. When you feel well enough to travel, we will return home."

Slarn laid back down. "What of Fiera and Morlithis?"

"We have heard nothing. The messengers did not inquire about them. Now get some rest. I will return shortly with food."

Slarn nodded, and Leo left the small hut, leaving Slarn to his thoughts.

***

Morlithis brought his bow up in front of him and dove for the smaller of his deadly foes, bringing his arrow point around to pierce the creature's side. The spiderlike creature snapped its three barbed tails down at Morlithis as he flung himself atop of the vicious creature, blocking two of the barbed tails with his bow, flinging it out, and pinning them down with his weight, but the third landed a jab into his armor. He felt the barb jab into his leather cuirass and silently praised the armor for yet again saving his life.

The spidery creature yanked its free tail back as it struggled against Morlithis's weight to free its other two tails while Morlithis shoved the tip of his arrow into the side of the creature's green, leaflike torso sack. It sank in easily, and the

167

spidery creature squirmed frantically, unintentionally making it easier for Morlithis to twist and turn his arrow deeper into the creature's bulbous side.

The beast stopped moving, and Morlithis felt the warm blood roll over his upper arm. Morlithis realized then that he had shoved the arrow deeper than he realized. He had sunken even his hand into the beast, its blood seeping down his numb forearm until he finally felt it on his upper arm.

He yanked his arm out, still holding his arrow, and scrambled off the dead creature, remembering the larger spiderlike beast.

He was too late to evade an attack, however. The creature sent its barbed tails into his back, and again his armor saved his life, but when the spiderlike beast didn't penetrate his armor, it sent one of its barbs into Morlithis's leg and yanked.

Morlithis screamed in agony as his leg erupted in pain, then screamed again as the creature yanked him around.

For the first time, Morlithis noticed the creature's teeth as it half screeched, half hissed at him. The beast's teeth swiveled into an upright position from their resting places inside the creature's mouth. Morlithis saw even the indentions that the teeth made from resting against the soft tissue of the beast's mouth. The teeth themselves were bloodstained and just as sharp as Kiernane teeth.

Morlithis saw the silklike webbing wafting out of two glands in the back of the spidery creature's mouth and knew that he was about to die, then he felt his hand. He felt his fingers move and felt the flora beneath them. He could move his hand now. He no longer had hold of the arrow, but he could feel it again. He still had the quiver on his back. He still had his bow in the other hand. He reached up behind his back, snatching an arrow as he brought his bow up, knocked an arrow, and loosed it.

The arrow sunk deep into the spidery creature's throat, and the beast stumbled backward, sending a fresh wave of agony through Morlithis's leg as it yanked its barbed tail free of him.

Morlithis fought through the pain, using it to focus his mind as he loosed another half dozen arrows into the creature's mouth as it stumbled back, and the beast plopped to the forest floor, dead.

Morlithis scanned the forest for any signs of other creatures and hobbled up to stand, noticing that his forearm had not yet regained its feeling. Then he saw the bloodstains on a patch of catnip.

"I wonder?" he whispered to himself and bent low, the pain in his leg erupting afresh. He yanked a leaf up and rubbed it on his forearm, instantly discovering a deep gash in his forearm as the numbing wore off. He bit through the newfound pain and rubbed more catnip on his wounded arm, stuffing as much as he could bear into his bleeding arm, then shoved several into his leg wound with a howl of pain.

Morlithis snatched a few more handfuls of catnip as he hobbled his way back to the riverbank, then crossed the chilly water and climbed back up onto the other side.

He decided that he would rest. He also decided that he would heed the warnings of others from now on.

Chapter seventeen

Morlithis sat against a tree, sipping on his waterskin just a few feet from the stream. He had left it at the riverbank when he crossed the river, and the first thing he did was snatch it up and then find the tree trunk to lean against.

It had only been a few minutes, but those few minutes gave him the rest that he needed to continue. Though he would rather rest longer, he still felt danger all around him and knew now that this place contained many unseen foes lurking about.

He found himself constantly searching the trees across the stream for more of the spidery beasts, but no matter how hard he looked, he could not see any, but he knew that did not mean that there were none there.

He finally gave up on a peaceful rest, settled for what he could get, and decided to continue home. He stood, topped off his waterskin, pulled his pack over his shoulders, and continued his trek. His shoulder throbbed, and stabbing pain ran along his upper leg with every step as he walked. The catnip helped to ease his wounds, but not much. Thankful to finally be near home, thankful that he was able to acquire more catnip, thankful that, somehow, his pack survived all his trials through the canyon, and thankful to be alive, he limped through the canyon, cringing with every movement, but found no more resistance.

***

Slarn gave himself a full day to heal and insisted the following morning that he was well enough to travel and, as Leo indeed saw that Slarn was doing better, though it was evident that his wound still needed healing, agreed to leave after the morning meal. Leo had already discussed returning to Cortin with a wartime party that was heading that way, tasked with announcing an official declaration of war.

***

Dawn came, and Morlithis awoke and packed his bedroll. He had made it into his people's lands near dusk the night before and found a well-hidden place to set camp under the long overhanging branches of a tree with branches that stretched out and sagged to the ground. This gave him good cover from any passing Kiernane. He also had a few mushrooms left in his pack to shield his scent. That and the potent aroma of his pack full of catnip would mask his scent well enough.

He knew that it didn't guarantee that anyone or anything still tracking him would not be able to find him, but it helped ease his mind enough that he could sleep. That, and the fact that he was exhausted, allowed sleep despite the danger and the pain from his wounds.

Now he was rested—as rested as he could be—and heading on his last leg of his journey home.

***

Slarn, Leo, and the messengers reached Cortin early that evening, discovering that Morlithis hadn't yet returned with the catnip, and Fiera found Leo after the village was summoned to the town meeting hall.

***

Morlithis reached the village, noticing the newly constructed barrier of wood pikes around the perimeter. As he neared the now-only entrance to the town, he heard someone yell to open the gate.

The newly constructed gate consisted of a thin wooden door that creaked as a single guard pulled it open.

"Help him to the healer!" ordered the same guard who Morlithis now saw standing above the gate on a platform. "I'll man the gate until you return."

The guard that opened the gate rushed to Morlithis's side, helping him as he walked. Morlithis noticed that the village streets were empty of occupants.

"Why are the streets so barren?" Morlithis asked the guard.

"The village has been summoned to the hall for an urgent announcement."

"I see. I have catnip for the priest-king. Is he still alive?"

"Yes, he still lives, but not for much longer."

Morlithis stopped walking. "My injuries can wait," he said, sliding off his pack. "Take this to the healer, quickly. It is catnip for the king."

174

The soldier nodded, taking the pack, and raced off to the healer's temple.

***

The town meeting was swift, taking only a few minutes for the messenger party to announce the war proclamation and pass along the directives that the high priest-king ordered for the villages in preparing for war, calling for the most skilled half of the hunters and trained fighters to report for duty in their capital city, Cryshtal.

***

Morlithis finally reached the healer's temple. It was instantly recognizable, as it was the second-largest building in the village, second only to the town meeting hall.

When he entered, he saw Slarn laying in a nearby bed with his wrist soaking in a green paste, which Morlithis knew to be a mixture of crushed catnip and healing paste that he had used only days ago. When mixed with the healing properties of catnip, the paste worked miracles and worked them very quickly.

Slarn, seeing Morlithis limping into the temple, jumped to his feet, rushing over to his friend's side.

"What happened to you?" he asked.

"It's a long story," Morlithis replied.

"Slarn!" hollered a red-and-white-striped Feleine, rushing over to them. "You must keep your wrist in the healing paste!" he yelled and grabbed Morlithis, guiding him to a vacant bed.

"Let me take a look at you," he said and gave Morlithis a once-over. "A wise decision to place catnip into your wounds. You are the one who retrieved it for us?"

"Yes," Morlithis replied as he fell onto the bed.

"Your priest-king thanks you. He will recover now that you have provided this abundance of catnip."

"Great," Morlithis replied, half-listening as he drifted off to sleep.

"Hmm. We will let him sleep," the healer said and turned to face Slarn. "You, my friend, must not remove your wrist from this paste," he said, walking over to Slarn. "You will be healed swiftly enough, thanks to your friend."

***

Fiera found Leo after the town meeting ended, and the two filled each other in on what had happened since they split up, Leo explaining that Slarn was in the healer's temple, and the two headed for the temple. They made their way through the crowds of Feleine warriors and hunters, gathering their supplies for their journey to the capital city. Those not preparing to leave prepared rations and stores to send along with their warriors. Only the most experienced villagers were tasked to fight, but the novice warriors and hunters went about their own tasks in preparing for their new responsibilities. It would be up to the few left behind to protect the villagers from the Kiernane threat if any packs threatened any of the villages. They would need to train harder, hunt better, and stay vigilant now that they were all drafted to defend the city, in addition to hunting for food. The village was changing, and not for the better.

***

Fiera and Leo entered the healer's temple, surprisingly finding Morlithis asleep in the bed across from Slarn.

Fiera rushed over to Slarn and hugged him.

Slarn nodded to Morlithis.

"It appears that he went through an ordeal," Slarn began, and Fiera and Leo looked over at Morlithis, seeing his wounds. "But it seems, as well, that he not only succeeded in bringing the catnip but accomplished—late as he was—beyond what we could have asked of him." Slarn pointed to a pile of catnip on the corner of the healer's worktable.

Fiera gasped.

Leo gazed with shock, recovering quickly, saying, "That is much more catnip than he left us with."

"Indeed, it is," Slarn replied.

"We will have to ask him about that when he wakes."

"And we will. For now, we prepare for war," Leo said. "When you two are better, the four of us will be heading to Cryshtal, the capital, to report for duty."

Join the Valley of Yeshen subscription to find out what happens

in season two and subsequent seasons.

https://www.cjkorrynserialsubscriptions.com/

Connect with C. J. Korryn

Learn more about C. J. Korryn at his author website, **cjkorryn.com** where you can sign up for his monthly newsletter, discover his other books, follow him on social media, and much more.

www.ingramcontent.com/pod-product-compliance
Lightning Source LLC
Chambersburg PA
CBHW070030260626
47159CB00005B/2003